A RITE OF PASSAGE

CHRISTOPHER J. HOLCROFT

OTHER TITLES BY
Christopher J. Holcroft

Only the Brave Dare
Canyon
Finding Thomas
One Last Concert
Time Voyager

A RITE OF PASSAGE

CHRISTOPHER J. HOLCROFT

DoctorZed
Publishing
www.doctorzed.com

This third edition published 2022 by DoctorZed Publishing.

DoctorZed Publishing books may be ordered through booksellers or by contacting:

DoctorZed Publishing
10 Vista Ave
Skye, South Australia 5072
www.doctorzed.com
61-(0)8 8431-4965

ISBN: 978-0-6455442-3-7 (sc)
ISBN: 978-0-6455442-2-0 (e)

A CIP number for this book is available at the National Library of Australia.

Cover image scuba diver © Jon Milnes | Dreamstime.com

Printed in Australia, UK & USA

DoctorZed Publishing rev. date: 02/08/2022

To my wife Yvonne,
for her everlasting love.

To youth everywhere…
live the adventure, and may you enjoy your
transition to adulthood.

"I learned that courage was not the absence of fear, but the triumph over it. The brave man is not he who does not feel afraid, but he who conquers that fear."

Nelson Mandela.

Chapter One

A thunderstorm had been building up all day. The clouds were low and heavy, and the wind had started blowing, but still, no rain fell. It didn't matter to the Venturers as they had organised a night snorkelling session a month ago. If necessary, they would change the calendar of events to suit the weather but not tonight. It didn't matter as they were going to get wet anyway.

Mike Hunter parked his car in the car park overlooking the Clovelly rock pool in Sydney's east. He had four Venturers with him, and they all alighted from the car to view the ocean at play. Cameron Wagstaff was one of Mike's former Venturers and was now in Rovers, the next age group up in scouting. He had volunteered to help Mike with adventurous activities and drove four other Venturers to the site. Yesterday the ocean was calm. Tonight it was on the boil. Waves rolled and crashed over the protective rock wall at the ocean end of the pool.

"I've never seen it like this before, Mike," Cameron said.

"This is supposed to be one of the city's safest rock pools for snorkelling and diving. However, looking at the outer rock wall there is a strong current surge over the wall."

"Cameron, now you appreciate why I need you here to act as our safety and rescue person.

"I'll get the boys to stay in the shallower end of the pool if you do the roving patrol on the perimeter."

"No probs Mike."

Mike and Cameron walked to the edge of the car park that overlooked the pool and showed the Venturers the boundaries for the night's swim.

"Our trouble is if we go past the halfway point set of stairs the pool gets quite deep," Mike said to the group.

"There are some great fish there, but the danger will be the current surge over the wall. Cameron is a good strong swimmer, but even he would have massive problems getting to you and bringing you back to shore if you get sucked over."

"How will we know when we're at the halfway point?" Ian, one of the Venturers asked.

"Fair question. You'll see a set of stairs halfway along the pool.

"Also, Cameron will be wearing his dive suit, face mask and snorkel so he can jump in and assist any of you if you need it. Cameron will have two glow sticks, a red one and a blue one attached to his snorkel. Don't go past him."

Mike had never taken this group of Venturers for a night swim before, especially in an ocean pool. He was prepared. Each boy was given a plastic luminous coloured glow stick which they had to bend to break the chemical phial inside, shake, and then attach to their snorkels. There would be three groups of swimmers and each group would have a different coloured glow stick. Orange for Mike's group, green for Peter's and blue for Mark's.

"So what sort of fish can we expect to find here," Peter, the Unit Chairman asked.

"You should see a variety of sea life from gropers to nudibranchs, Fortescue's, catfish and our deadly blue-ringed octopus," Mike said.

"What's the problem with the octopus?" Ian asked.

"This style of octopus looks very pretty with its multiple blue rings, but if it bites you, then chances are you will die within a very short time."

"Okay! Don't play with the octopussies."

"Also, don't forget. If you see a small shark, it will probably be a Port Jackson. They're harmless, so don't panic," Cameron said.

"On the wall under the surf club that overlooks the pool, you'll find a large metal poster with photos of the marine life and a description.

"It's worth a look on the way in and out of the pool. Remember, like you, Mike and I aren't fish experts."

Scott looked at both Mike and Cameron.

"But you are both divers, aren't you?"

"What's your point?"

"Well you both should know a lot about fish, shouldn't you?"

"Scott, we know how to safely scuba dive and what to do in emergencies. We have an idea of some fish, but not all. Places like this surf club recognise that sort of lack of knowledge of most people – divers included. That's why they erected the metal sign below."

Mike was becoming impatient. He could see the huge

bulbous clouds being blown onshore and felt the air pressure change approaching. The Venturer Leader reckoned he had around one and half hours before the car park would be awash with heavy rain.

"Okay fellows. Let's change, gear up and have a look at the sign," Mike said.

"We're running out of time before the storm hits."

"You're not worried about getting wet?" Ian asked.

"Yes and no. Yes, I am afraid of getting wet when we are out of the water and want to get changed before going home. No, I'm not afraid of getting wet and going for a swim in the rain. However, I don't like damp smelly cars or the chance of swimming in the pool during any lightning activity."

The boys all agreed and quickly changed into their "spring" suits; dive suits with short sleeves and legs. The boys were split into their various groups and given their respective glow sticks to activate and place on their snorkels. Within five minutes the group was ready to snorkel.

It was almost a scene from a movie watching the group walk from the car park down the various steps and ramps to the pool. The multi-coloured dive suits and bright glow sticks gave a surreal effect to the night sky. The boys stopped for a brief moment to view the photos of the various marine life that has been found in the rock pool. They then made their way down to the shallow end of the pool to put their fins and snorkels on and enter the water. Each snorkeler had some form of a waterproof torch.

Mike split the boys into their various groups and they all

started swimming slowly around the pool searching the rocky, sandy bottom for signs of any marine life.

Occasionally some of the boys would stop and dive under for closer views of the various fish. Cameron had also suited up and walked around the pool's edge to the halfway point.

He wanted no issues tonight. A look from the halfway point to the rock wall showed he and Mike were right. Large waves bombarded the wall and created a tidal surge in one corner. Any swimmer caught in the surge could be lost over the wall and sucked out to sea. Cameron hopefully would not swim tonight. If he did, it meant he was trying to save one of the Venturers or stopping them from being sucked out to sea.

"Have a go at that!" Scott said to Brett.

"There's a couple of sharks down there and they seem to be mating."

"Where?"

"Near the large rock overhang. Check it out."

The boys went back under the surface and played their torches around the base of the rock. Sure enough, Scott was right. There were four small sharks playing games or mating with each other. The Venturers seemed more excited than the sharks themselves. They returned to the surface for more air and were spotlighted by Cameron and his torch. Cameron put his two hands to the top of his head. It was the diver's signal for "Okay" from someone on the surface. The boys had been briefed that if asked by any of their group tonight with this signal they had to answer immediately.

Scott stopped and returned the "Okay" signal to Cameron. The teenager then showed four fingers before putting the palms of both his hands together and opening and closing the fingers. Cameron laughed. He knew Scott was telling him there were four Port Jackson sharks under the water.

The Rover then checked Mike and the third group. All returned the "Okay" sign and kept snorkelling.

Cameron was one of Mike's former Venturers and had completed his top award under his leader's tutelage and also had many adventures. It was fun seeing a new group of teenage boys having some of the same fun. Ordinarily, Cameron and the rest of his Rover Crew would only have a few outings a year with the Venturers and Mike. Scott changed all that.

Scott had been in the Unit for two years and created international headlines with two major incidents. The first involved being taken prisoner with the rest of his Unit by a group of Russian Mafia as the Russians were trying to retrieve packages of heroin to flood Sydney streets. The heroin had been dropped off by a Russian mother ship to an abandoned submarine hulk the boys had gone to explore. When the Venturers and the land-based Russians met at the submarine, the mafia decided to take the boys prisoner rather than shoot them all. That was the beginning of their problems. The Russians took Mike and the boys to a nearby abandoned convict jail turned into a lighthouse and locked them up.

Scott escaped from his cell and turned the lighthouse into a weapon against the Russian Mafia who were caught in a combined operation by Police and the Defence Force.

Cameron kept scouring the water and checking on the boys and Mike. All was safe.

The second time Scott made international headlines was

only a few months ago when he went canyoning with this same group of Venturers up on the Alexander Plateau in the Blue Mountains. One of the Venturers was attacked by two Peregrine falcons when he was abseiling on an open rock ledge and ended up jumping back first into a tree to escape the birds of prey. The Venturer, Brett, was impaled. Scott abseiled into the tree, separated Brett from the branch impaling him and held him in the tree until rescue help arrived. If that wasn't enough, as he was climbing out of one of the canyons, a Rover fell through the canyon roof and Scott stopped him mid-fall and saved his life. The Rover had fallen heavily on Scott and tore the teenager's right interior ligaments of his leg.

Scott limped as far as he could out of the canyons before being piggybacked on the last leg of the journey. He was recognised for his double bravery act by the country's Governor General and became Australia's first National Youth of the Year. He had already been honoured with his State's highest civilian award for bravery for his work in rescuing Mike and his fellow Venturers from the Russian Mafia.

Before the double rescue, Scott was instrumental in setting up the National Rover Emergency Rescue Service modelled on a similar scheme in Canada. The Rovers, all aged between 17 and 26, who helped rescue Scott and Brett, were part of Scott's scheme he set up.

Cameron was an active member in his Regional Rover activities and had been quietly instructed by the national body of Rovers to assist Mike on adventurous activities where Scott would be involved.

The Rovers had placed an invisible ring of support around

the teenager while he was in Venturers. This was unheard of and was not to be made public.

Slowly, each of the Venturer groups started approaching the halfway point in the Clovelly rock pool. Cameron was on edge, not worried so much, just highly alert. He shone his dive torch on each of the groups and pointed them back to the shallow end. Each complied, but each also pushed the boundary of how far they could go. Cameron smiled when he realised what the boys were doing. After all, he had done the same thing when he was a Venturer with Mike.

The wind had picked up and the first spits of rain started falling. The dark clouds were almost directly overhead. Cameron flashed Mike and pointed to his watch and then the sky. Mike responded by checking his watch and giving the "Okay" sign.

It happened quite quickly. An extraordinarily tall wave crashed over the rocky barrier to the pool sending a giant pressure surge toward the boys. No sooner had Cameron given the Okay sign than a wave hit with the force of a small plane crashing into the water.

Brett was the first to see the pressure surge heading towards the Venturers and started yelling out and flashing his torch towards each of the groups. Mike looked up in horror as he saw the giant wall of water heading toward him and the boys. Cameron froze. There was nothing he could do except watch the effect on the boys and then dive in and pull back any boys that began to be sucked back out to sea.

One by one, each of the groups heard Brett and dived under the surface. Mike was the last to make the dive. Cameron was rooted to the edge of the pool. The pressure surge sent a giant wave throughout the pool. The boys and Mike started surfacing again as the surge hit the shoreline and started making its way back to the pool entrance. Again the Venturers dived quickly under the surface and made their way to the pool floor. The surge passed overhead and the Venturers started bopping around the surface again to get air.

Cameron signalled the group to ensure all were safe. He doubled check the count of "Okay" signs and then signalled for the group to exit the pool. The boys swam and bobbed their way to Cameron and slowly made their way out of the pool and gathered in front of the giant metal poster of marine life.

"That was close!" Brett said as he started making his way out of the pool.

"You did well with your signalling and going back under," Cameron said. "You helped the others avert what could have been a major problem for them. Well done."

The other Venturers gathered around Brett on the pool promenade.

"Well done, Brett. That was a good signalling effort out there with the pressure surge," Mike said.

"Yeah. Well done, Brett," Scott said as he broke out into a laugh.

"It's a pleasure hearing another end to Mike's phrase of "Well done".

The Venturers joined in laughing as they saw Mike look uncomfortable. It was great to know someone else received plaudits, not just Scott. The boys moved along the promenade to the large metallic fish poster.

"I hope the Rovers and Venturers participating in the Centenary Sailing Regatta in a few weeks don't have these sorts of issues," Cameron said. "If they do, I hope they keep as level-headed as you lot."

Mark looked perplexed. He looked briefly at Mike and then to Cameron. "What's the Centenary Sailing Regatta?"

"This is where hundreds of Rovers and Venturers will gather in Botany Bay and sail every sort of craft they can in some controlled races," Cameron said with a smile. "We decided to get the Crews and Units to all go sailing where the activity was close to Sydney."

"Yeah, but where does the centenary part come in?"

"Oh yeah. To celebrate 100 years since the start of Scouting in Australia, several Rover Crews decided to hold a major activity in a prime location. We wanted to not only fly our Rover flag but also to help recruit from Venturer ranks and the general public.

"There will be masses of scouting people there so it should be a big event."

Mike saw the faces of his Ventures and chimed in. "Our boats haven't been registered in a while, so we'll have to see if we go or not. Don't get tied around the axles yet."

Scott read his leader's face and decided to break an awkward moment. "That's it. That's the one we saw," the blonde-haired youth said as he pointed to the photo of a groper on the wall underneath the surf club. "The damn thing kept following us around."

"You missed Mike feeding the groper," Mark said.

"I didn't think the fish was that friendly?"

"Ah yes, but Mike fed it some sea urchin."

"Alright, I'm hooked. I never saw Mike or anyone else take fish food to the pool with you."

Mike and Cameron started laughing.

"Scott, when you do your scuba diving course you'll see why Cameron and I carry knives on our legs," Mike said.

"It's not to kill big scary marine life, but help out with gentle things like feeding our big groper."

"What did you feed it?" Scott asked.

"I opened some sea urchin. These are little spiky marine life that attaches themselves to rock surfaces.

"Inside, their bright yellow flesh becomes an instant attractant to other fish. It's sort of like a delicacy and fish like the groper will feed out of your hands."

"Wow. Okay, okay, I'll talk to mum and dad about the dive course and see if I can do it."

"Me too," said Mark.

"Hang on, don't forget me," Brett said as he sidled up to Scott and Mark.

"We should have enough people for the course by now."

Cameron looked at Mike and smiled. He was just as keen as these Venturers when he was their age. Snorkelling was fine but nothing beat the freedom of scuba diving.

"I'll check with the dive shop this weekend and see what discount rates they can give us," Mike said.

"It's time we did another course and started exploring some wrecks and forts."

"We need to have this discussion," Scott said. "I'm pretty keen."

"Scott, I'll get some facts and figures on the next dive course and get back to you soon. In the meantime, we all need to get back to the cars and get changed as it's about to storm."

The group hurriedly made their way back to the car park just as the heavens opened and it started raining. Mike sidled up to Scott and thanked him for talking about the groper when he did. Scott just smiled and kept walking.

Brett was the first out of his wetsuit. He started wiping himself down and bent forward to wipe his feet. The scars on his back where he had been impaled on a tree during his infamous canyoning trip with the Unit had healed nicely. Scott couldn't help but look at the scars. After all, he was instrumental in Brett being alive today to show the surgical leftover. The rest of the boys quickly stripped off their wetsuits and got changed before piling into the two cars for the return journey to their scout hall and parent pick-ups.

Scott's mind raced as he thought of the adventures and new challenges scuba diving could open for him. Being able to stay under the surface for some time and explore the ocean floor, feed fish and see the larger sea animals up close and personal were exciting ideas. He also toyed with images in his mind of himself as a marine biologist after he left school and university. First, he needed the scuba course under his belt so he could taste what one possible future would be for himself. He stopped in mid-thought and started thinking whether his Unit should be participating in the Centenary Sailing Regatta or leave it to the Rovers.

He decided to leave it to the Rovers. This was their gig.

Chapter Two

Ken turned on the radio and started to laugh. He'd heard it all before. Another crackdown! Sure! How long will this one last? The announcer said the NSW Police Commissioner had announced a crackdown on outlaw motorcycle gangs in Sydney.

"A multi-agency police strike force has been set up to combat escalating violence between rival Sydney motorcycle gangs.

"Commissioner Rex Small said several shootings, arson attacks and assaults have taken place over the past two months in and around Sydney involving motorcycle gang members.

"He said the violence is related to a turf war involving drug distribution networks in inner-city nightclubs and burgeoning racketeering among shopkeepers …"

Ken reached across his bed to the bedside table and picked up his mobile phone. He dialled his lieutenant, Roger.

"Mate, did you hear the news about another copper crackdown on us?"

"Yeah. It won't last. Someone's complaining within the nightclub scene and some of our local shops about having to pay us some money."

"The hide of them!"

"Yeah. I thought so too. Geoff and Ted will scout around today to try and find out who's spilling their guts."

"Okay. If you need the boys, just let me know and we'll call a meeting ... inside the nightclub."

"Okay."

Ken was the head of the Raven Motorcycle Club which had been having a turf war with its rival gang, the Eagles, for the past two years. Both gangs had been trying to raise money any way they could to outfit their clubs with the latest high-tech security and best motorbikes. This included selling drugs on the streets and in nightclubs, along with standover protection rackets among shopkeepers. Police had tried to infiltrate the two gangs for some time with little luck. It was also hard to find something wrong with Ken as he ran a legitimate motorcycle sales and repair business. This was a great way for the Ravens to launder some of their illegal money.

Ken had four shipping containers delivered to a property he owned just south of Sydney. The Ravens toiled tirelessly in organising earth-moving equipment to help dig a series of underground tunnels on the property and then burying two of the containers over a series of days.

The Ravens' alternate headquarters was complete. The two containers above ground contained legitimate motorcycle parts and accessories for Ken's business. The two underground provided space for private club meetings and storage for any equipment including weapons. The containers above ground also allowed for legitimate access to the property by club members for motorcycle part swap meets. Membership was varied among the two clubs. Some people were involved in community organisations including rifle clubs. Police found it very hard to discern who were motorcycle gang members and who were not ... except on chapter riding days and rallies when members would wear their club colours as a vest over their leather jackets. These were special days when each of the clubs would take to the streets and highways on their bikes in a large show of strength. When Police intelligence officers found out about the rides, undercover police in unmarked cars would shadow the gang members.

On one occasion Police found out about a Raven's ride of around 60 bikers from Sydney to the southern state border of Victoria. Police set up a special roadblock that funnelled the bikers to a side road. Then, each biker was forced to stop in line and Police on the side filmed each biker and their machine. The move agitated the bikers but they could do nothing about it as they were outnumbered by a large Police presence.

Ken felt under his bed for his Steyer rifle. Good. It was still there. The virtually all plastic semi-automatic assault rifle was used by several western Armies as a front-line weapon for its soldiers. It was nice to have people with international munitions connections in the Ravens. They had access to weapons from overseas and could obtain some if push came to shove and things hotted up in a turf war. Ken's trusty weapon had been imported in parts from overseas in containers full of motorcycle engines and spares. A club member who was a former armourer put the weapon together. Ken kept a small array of weapons near him including baseball bats and over-large spanners. Twice, he had been the subject of attacks by members of the Eagles. Twice, he had managed to get to his weapons and return fire before the shooters fled. Eventually, he knew his luck would run out. The mobile phone rang. Ken checked the number of the caller. If he didn't know the caller, he would let the call go to the message bank. It was Tim.

"G'day mate. We need to talk. Are you free this afternoon?"

"Yeah, mate."

"Excellent. See you at 5 pm in the chamber."

"Done."

The calls were always short, sharp, and cryptic. You never knew who was listening and why. Tim was like most other members of the Ravens. He worked part-time and was available as required to attend club business, as and when it arose. His loyalty was to the club first and then his family. There could be no deviation and nor would the club countenance it. He had been scouting for a new meeting place and storage area for the Ravens as the two underground containers the club used were slowly becoming stuffy and mouldy.

Tim worked part-time for the National Parks as a tour guide. His job was to take schools and other groups on tours of historical landmarks taken over by the National Parks Service. This included an old whaling station, Army sites no longer in service and sites that the First Fleet headed by Captain Arthur Phillip had used two centuries ago. He knew his way around most historical parts of Sydney the Parks Service looked after including some of the lighthouses. Tim had become excited when he found out the National Parks was no longer going to be looking after Cook Island, just south of Sydney. Its management was to be transferred to the National Trust. Cook Island was a former Army hospital site from the 1800s.

It was originally built as a fort to help ward off possible invading forces from Russia and then used as a base to stop smugglers entering and leaving Botany Bay. The Russians never came, and the original canons were never fired in anger. The site was built on a huge rock base around 500 metres offshore, so it had a natural moat. A wooden bridge connected Cook Island to the mainland. The Army had built a series of ammunition chambers on the island so it could fire a couple of large cannons pointing out to sea to repel any invaders. The problem was in the construction. No sooner had the island fort been built that it started to show signs of decay.

The Federal Government of the time had used a dodgy construction company to build the fort and it had used a lot of substandard materials. Several ongoing partial rebuilds had to be carried out to various chambers and accommodation areas. Eventually, any threat of invasion of Australia subsided. A new and better port service was built in Botany Bay and Cook Island lay idle for some time. The Federal Government handed over the island to the State Government and the National Parks became the maintainer of the place and ran organised tours. To make money, the National Parks even allowed weddings to be held on the island as it had spectacular views of Botany Bay and its surrounds for the subsequent photo shoots. Now the island was again going into disrepair and the cost of maintenance was prohibitive.

Cook Island was situated at the end of a peninsula. A large sloping hill overlooked the entrance to the island and had a lone sandstone tower on it. When the military built its fort, it also built the sentry tower so soldiers could warn of anyone approaching the island by road. The tower had three levels, a ground-floor reception and ablution area; a first-floor sleeping area and an open battlement area for the soldiers to walk around, regardless of the weather. The tower itself was the shape of a corner of a castle. It could easily be mistaken for a lone chess piece from a distance. The National Parks had only opened the tower for special occasions and tours. Now, it too was in disrepair internally and was being closed.

The clock struck 4.30 pm and it was time for Tim to finish work for the day. He changed out of his bush green-coloured pants and brown shoes; took off his dark green pullover and light-yellow shirt and placed them all in his locker. He reached in and pulled out his thick-heeled black boots, jeans, T-shirt, leather vest, helmet, and gloves. Within minutes the transformation was complete. Tim had gone from a tour guide to a fully-fledged biker. He was now a Raven, once more. The sound of Tim's Harley Davidson motorcycle bursting into life only turned a few heads from passing pedestrians. The 1200cc machine was quieter than most bikes but could erupt into a speed machine within a heartbeat. Riding the 1200cc bike set Tim apart from other riders. He had a machine the envy of a lot of riders. Then again, Tim did not own his own house, nor did he have a wife and children or own a car. Tim's second love was his $26,000 bike. His first was the Ravens.

Tim rode out to the Ravens' bunker on Ken's property. The ride itself was uneventful and left a smug look on Tim's face. He could glide in and out of the traffic on his motorcycle and make his way ahead of most vehicles. This action sometimes caused several motorists to gesture rudely to him as he left cars in his wake. Generally, Police left him alone but checked his license plate to confirm the bike was not stolen or that any arrest warrants were outstanding. Tim entered Ken's property. He couldn't help himself. The moment he drove through the reinforced steel gates Tim looked to his right and smiled. He knew Ken would be watching him on a monitor. Tim drove to the rear of the property where two shipping containers were parked side by side with a canvas canopy joining them. One of the containers was open and held a huge array of motorcycle parts in all sorts of shapes and colours. The other was closed. Tim switched off his motorcycle and kicked down the stand. He took off his helmet and stood up to meet his club President.

"G'day mate," Tim said as he pulled off his gloves and extended his right hand for Ken to shake.

"Hi Tim."

Ken shook hands with Tim and then placed his left hand around Tim's shoulder. Both men walked into the open shipping container. Ken pulled down a canvas cover over the entrance to thwart prying eyes.

"What's up mate?"

"Ken, I think I have found a fantastic place for a new headquarters if we need one."

"What's wrong with this one?"

"Nothing a lot of fresh air, space and parking couldn't fix."

Both men made their way to the rear of the container. Instinctively, Ken reached to the floor and pulled up a ring bolt attached to a trap door. The two men made their way down a set of dimly lit stairs and then lowered the trap door after them. Ken turned on a powerful overhead light and air conditioning system before the two sat down on a set of comfortable lounge chairs in the underground chamber.

"Mate, you know I work all around Sydney with National Parks," Tim said.

"Well, I think I have found a great place for a headquarters or a place to stage a battle if one ever erupts with the Eagles."

"Okay, I'll bite. What are we talking about?"

"National Parks is about to give up Cook Island and ..."

"Where or what is Cook Island?"

Tim took Ken through the history of Cook Island and brought him up to date with moves by the State Government to close the old fort.

"It's perfect for us," Tim said.

"We can park opposite the island along the peninsula. We can post a lookout in the old sentry tower and if need be, bring in or take out any special equipment by water at night."

"Tim, isn't Cook Island on a ring road on top of a peninsular?"

"Yes."

"If anything happened to us there we'd be bottled up."

Tim thought for a few moments. "Ken, if we needed to we could ride onto the island and around to the point where a boat and floating platform could be anchored for a sea getaway."

Ken laughed. "You try and think of everything."

"Not only that but there is a pub almost opposite and a couple of great cafes."

"Just what do you think is happening with the Eagles, Tim? You speak as if a war is about to break out between us both."

"Mate, I've been reading the signs. We've had a number

of our shop owners and businesses asked to pay the Eagles as well as us; a couple of our blokes were king hit from behind at a pub last month, their bikes damaged and some of the girls we are using in Kings Cross are being harassed by goons that look awfully like Eagle boys."

"Yes. We're not doing too well at the moment I admit. Our business franchises are being eaten into by the Eagles.

"Also, Trevor and Damian both copped a good hiding after being hit from behind and their bikes cost heaps to fix. I need more information about our girls at Kings Cross to start tying up all loose ends.

"I think you are right. We'd be fools to think the Eagles are not trying to push into our territory and angle for a takeover."

"Ken, we should call a full Chapter meeting and see what the other members know is happening. Then, we should work out what steps we need to take against the Eagles."

The men went on to discuss ordinary club issues over a few cold beers. The underground containers were a bit stuffy, but the cool and shade helped keep the fridge cold. After forty minutes the meeting was over and the men made their way back to the container above them and out into the sunlight.

"Ok, Tim. All is set. I'll call a meeting here for next Monday night."

"Okay, Ken. I'll have some more information for you by then."

Tim donned his helmet and gloves. He got on his bike, kicked the stand up and started the engine. Within seconds Tim was on his way home. He had other Raven business to do. By day, Tim was seen with short hair in his State Public Service job as he dealt with the general public. However, by night, it was a different story as Tim would wear a wig with unkempt, dark brown straggly hair. The wig did not necessarily hide Tim's identity, but helped confuse onlookers. Tim rode to his rented brick home on the southern outskirts of Sydney and parked on the front lawn. He didn't take his helmet off before he entered because he was wary of intruders. Tim checked the locks on his door and saw they were correctly in place. It was safe to enter. He walked down his hallway and into his study so he could check his facsimile machine. Two faxes were waiting for him and he scanned them quickly.

The first fax was from fellow Raven, Trevor, who wanted to join him for a ride in a few hours. The second was from Damian with a similar message. The Ravens did not use their mobile phones too often in case they were monitored by Police.

"Well, it looks like the stage is set for a fun night," Tim said to himself. It was time to check what equipment he needed.

Tim went to his study and opened a drinks cabinet. Behind a false wall at the rear of the cabinet, he retrieved a flexible heavy rubber cosh, a couple of large plastic cable ties and a flick knife.

The cosh was excellent as a weapon to bludgeon people and knock them senseless. It fitted neatly inside his jacket and could be easily retrieved. The plastic cable ties are usually used by Police as makeshift handcuffs and were nigh impossible to break, especially if the victim's hands were tied behind their backs. He put the ties down the rear of his jeans. The flick knife was a close-quarter handy weapon. Tim never used handguns as the people he harassed were quite willing to submit to what he wanted without their use. He put the knife in his right boot. Tim was ready. Well, almost. He strode into his bedroom and picked up his wig and put it on his head. A quick look in the mirror to adjust the wig and he was now ready.

Tim donned his helmet and gloves and hopped back on his motorcycle. He had a mission to accomplish; to help bring a constant flow of money into the Ravens' coffers. The ride into Kings Cross was uneventful and Tim met up with fellow Ravens, Trevor and Damian. The trio parked around two blocks from where they were about to unleash their anger at shop owners and businesses who were not paying their 'dues' for protection by the Ravens.

Tim was the first to enter the 24-hour nightclub. Trevor stayed near the door and Damian followed close behind Tim. The trio knew this club well.

They had visited it several times to 'talk' with the owner Theo, a Greek businessman. Tim and Damian made their way through the dimly lit passageway leading into the main lounge area. The pair split as they walked either side of a row of bar tables and chairs and made their way to the right-hand extremity of the room. Around 20 people were drinking, talking and listening to the ever-loud music being piped through the ceiling speakers. The duo met up again as they walked to a door flanked outside by two security guards.

"We need to see Theo," Tim said as he went to walk past the guards.

One of the guards barred his way while the second said their boss was not in. Tim moved swiftly and with surgical precision. He drove his right hand to the guard's throat and simultaneously kicked the man's feet from under him. Damian was just as quick. He grabbed the second guard's right hand, stretched it out and turned it at the wrist making it completely useless. He then drove a hard kick under the man's armpit, dislocating his arm and sending him to the ground in a screaming heap. Tim finished his man with a heavy strike to the side of the head that left the guard unconscious. The game was on. Damian pulled out a small iron bar he had under his coat and leveraged the door handle until the door sprang open.

Both men then made their way into the inner sanctum of Theo's bar and grille. Ahead was a second door with a camera above it. The room was dimly lit and was decorated with mirrors. Damian reached into his coat pocket and pulled out a maritime flare. He cracked the end and set off the bright luminous rescue candle. The sudden bright light in front of the camera blocked all vision by the camera operator and shrouded the room in ebbing bright red light and smoke. Tim used Damian's iron bar and smashed the lock on the door. Damian then kicked it open and ran inside to confront a large Greek man with long wavy locks dressed in a black shirt, trousers and shoes. It was a scene from a Zorro film, only there was no straight brimmed hat, large gloves and whip to be seen.

"Tim, you have no right to be in here," Theo said as he walked towards a table with two drawers.

"Theo, the Ravens understand you have been holding out on us and doing some business with the Eagles instead!"

"That's not true. I have paid you generously, for your protection."

"The Ravens haven't received last week's payment and are getting worried you are about to change allegiances. We thought we would pay you a little visit to remind you of our services and of the help we offer you.

"Oh, by the way, your boys out front may need some looking to after we have gone."

Theo looked worried. He was a man about to make a decision. Either way, he lost to those standover men. In the left drawer was a wad of money he could pay off these bikies and hopefully carry on without being injured. In the right drawer was a .38 calibre Smith and Wesson handgun. The question was, could he get to the right drawer without much ado and survive. Damian read Theo's body language and pulled out his revolver as Theo placed his right hand on the right drawer.

"No, Theo. Not that one," Damian said. "Try the other one, real slow."

Theo began to sweat as he realised he had taken too long to make the decision. Next time he'll wear a vest with a handgun under his armpit or buy a spring lever derringer that fitted under his sleeve and was activated by pressing his forearm against his body, thus delivering the tiny weapon straight into his hand – Wild West style.

"You won't get away with this," Theo blurted out as he slowly pulled the left drawer open.

"We are and we will. We are here for your protection against any gangsters who try and hurt you," Damian said with a leer.

Both Ravens noticed the large wad of money in the drawer. Tim walked closer and helped Theo open the drawer wide.

"Mate, we're going to do you a favour," Tim said.

"We'll only take what's due and leave you with the rest. If that's not honest, what is?"

Theo took out a roll of money. He counted the extortion amount the Ravens wanted for last week and this week and handed the notes to Tim.

"I'll let the boys know to keep a special look out on this place," Tim said.

"We don't want any nasty Eagle boys hanging around. After all, they could cause you grief."

Tim put the money in his vest pocket and both he and Damian left the room. They walked past the two security guards who were still on the ground. One was out cold and the other was writhing in pain. When the guard saw the Ravens coming toward him, he cringed.

"Have nothing to fear from us," Damian said.

"Play the game right and you'll be okay."

The guard nodded and the Ravens made their way out through the drinks lounge. Patrons turned their backs on the pair so they would not be involved. Theo's bar and grille was a great place for a drink and to pick up bar girls. No use spoiling a good night. Trevor had stopped several patrons from entering the premises on the pretext there was a fire being investigated inside. Across the road in an open piazza-style courtyard, a man dressed in an off-white shirt and coat sat drinking coffee and watching Trevor. He had a laptop with a USB internet connection and was typing away. He looked like an up-market salesman or a yuppie trying to show off. Trevor saw the man but paid little attention to him.

Damian and Tim joined Trevor and the three walked hurriedly around the block to their bikes and quickly took off. They rode to Damian's place via a lap around his suburb to ensure they weren't being followed. The three rode their bikes up the side passage to Damian's bungalow and parked them out of sight.

"I think Theo will wise up and keep paying us on time," Tim said.

"I don't," Damian said.

"He was prepared to bring grief on himself tonight. I could see him weighing up which drawer to open.

"What would you have done?"

"I had the handpiece pointed at his hand and would have shot him through his palm."

"Yes, that would have slowed him down …"

"And probably brought every cop in Kings Cross into his bar," Trevor said.

"I saw several cops taking their fat Sergeants for their nightly patrol. They wouldn't go in unless they had good backup."

Tim looked Trevor in the eye.

"Why? How come they wouldn't go in if called?" Tim asked.

"They are quite scared of being involved in any gangland war that could break out if they barge in and arrest the wrong people. That's why.

"Also, word seems to have got around that bad blood is brewing between us and the Eagles. We pulled off our extortion tonight. My question is, how long can this last before either the shopkeepers and business owners wise up, the Police become involved en masse or we bump into some of the Eagle boys and have to fight on the spot.

"It's like a set of storm clouds gathering. Eventually, we will have to change our tactics or face a fight we won't be prepared for … and then lose out on our weekly takings."

Damian and Tim stood rooted to the ground. This was the first time Trevor had gone into such detail about his feelings of what was happening around the Ravens.

"You are right," Damian said.

"We need to meet at Ken's and look at where we are and whether we can change how we do business to get us a better break."

Both Tim and Trevor agreed. The three went into Damian's home and had a round of beers. After all, $10,000 for a 20-minute workout at Theo's was not bad going.

Within the hour, the Eagles had photos of Tim, Damian and Trevor. The man sitting opposite Theo's with his laptop had taken images of the three Ravens entering and leaving the bar. He uploaded the photos to his laptop and after tethering his mobile phone to the computer, sent them direct to the Eagles headquarters. Eagles president Rick Lane was amused. He had been spoiling for a fight with the Ravens for some time and needed an excuse to launch action against his rivals.

He now had it.

Chapter Three

Scott sat in his room and counted his money. He had done enough jobs gardening for his mother Kelly and babysitting for neighbours, to do the dive course. His father Allan wanted him to save the money for his first car. Scott's idea was to gain new skills that could be bankable at a later time, maybe … also, to have some new adventures. After all, hiking, canoeing, abseiling and surfing were becoming so ho-hum for the teenager. Scott needed a new challenge and a new playground.

Scott filled out his dive course forms and went to the lounge room to talk with his parents. He needed their overall permission to undertake the course and to organise a medical check to ensure he had no problems with his ears, sinuses and breathing passages. It took a bit of "sweet talking" between Scott and his parents, but they eventually agreed to consent to him undertaking the course. The car could go on hold for a while.

"Thanks, dad, mum," Scott said.

"This will open up a new world to explore and give me some great skills."

"Gee Scott, I can't imagine who you are trying to emulate with your skills base," Allan said.

"Dad, I'm not out to try and match or better Mike. I just want to explore as much of this world as I can, while I can.

"How will I ever know how to leave a better world in time

to come, if I don't know what shape it is in now? At least this way, I get to see what life is like underwater from some reasonable depths. I guess this will make my birthdays and Christmas so much easier for everyone too as there will be many things for them to choose from that I could use in my activities."

"Like what?"

Scott couldn't help smiling as he drew a deep breath before continuing.

"Oh, you know, a camera with an underwater housing, a wet suit or some good abseiling gear."

"Go to bed Scott. This current course of yours will cost a packet as it is."

"Good night mum. Good night dad," Scott said with a large smile as he made his way back to his bedroom.

Mission accomplished. Now for the course. Better still, let the adventure begin.

The Venturer's dive course was conducted upstairs of the dive shop over several nights. This included theory lessons and familiarisation with the dive equipment. Scott, Mark and Brett were looking forward to starting the practical part of the course. Skip, the shop owner organised to take the boys to a shallow beach area in Botany Bay. The boys practised donning and doffing their wetsuits; buoyancy compensator devices; attaching their air bottles and checking the pressure gauges.

"There seems quite a lot of things to check just to get under the water," Mark said.

"Yes," Skip said.

"But if you stuff up here on land, you'll probably die

underwater. That's why we go over and over these basic operations, so they become second nature to you.

"We want you to have a great experience underwater and to return with a smile on your face to tell the tale."

Skip then gently took hold of Mark's instrument pack and turned it upside down. He pointed to the air tank and told Mark to turn it on. Immediately the airline went hard and a sizzling sound could be heard as air rushed from the tank and down the line.

"Remember. If you have the instrument panel facing upwards, air pressure could crack the panel sending glass into your face before you have any time to react," Skip said.

The other boys ensured their instrument panels faced downwards, without a word being spoken. Skip took the boys into the water once their equipment had been donned correctly and checked. The fun began when he signalled each of the boys, in turn, to take off and replace their face masks underwater at a depth of around three metres. Skip arranged the boys in a circle with everyone kneeling, so all were in view of each other. Mark was the first. Skip gave Mark the "Okay" sign which the youth responded to. The instructor then signalled for Mark to take off and replace his mask.

Mark started taking off his mask and his eyes began to bulge. His movements were in slow motion as he tried to replace his mask. He positioned the mask on his face and then placed his left hand at the top of the face plate. His right hand went over his nose and pinched it tight. The youth then started to blow air into his mask to force the water out. The problem was a small fish had become trapped in Mark's mask and it looked like the boy was stuck inside a fishbowl with a fish darting back and forth across the mask. Scott and Brett couldn't hold it in any longer and started laughing. This was not an easy task underwater, with a mouthpiece in your mouth. Brett laughed and coughed as he took in water. Scott bit down harder on his mouthpiece to stop any water from entering his mouth. The scene of the fish in Mark's mask, Brett coughing and spluttering underwater and Skip trying to keep a straight face sent Scott into large fits of laughing. The boy turned over and over in somersaults. It was a moment Scott would treasure for the rest of his days.

Skip helped Brett first to regain his breath and then to calm down. He then signalled Mark to take off and replace the mask again. Scott returned to the circle with a giant grin. He didn't dare laugh again. Mark ensured there were no freeloaders in his mask this time and completed the operation perfectly. Scott was next. He held back a series of giggles but completed the task effortlessly. Brett initially had trouble keeping his eyes open but soon got the hang of it and calmed sufficiently to also complete the task. The underwater course seemed to be a tradition starting within the Venturer Unit with most of the Venturers with their PADI cards. These enabled the youths to fill up their air tanks at virtually any dive shop globally and hire dive equipment. Scott, Mark, and Brett were the last of the current Venturers to undergo the training.

It didn't take Mark long to have the last laugh. Skip had the boys swim around for a few minutes at a depth of around five metres and then signalled them to form a circle on their knees. The next procedure was easy. Skip undid his weight belt and dropped it to the ocean floor. He then picked it up, placed it on his back and leant forward. His hands found the strap and buckle and he connected the two, pulled the strap tight and pushed hard on the buckle to lock it into place. He knelt upright and gave the "Okay" sign. Each boy replied "Okay" in turn.

Skip then signalled to Scott to take off his weight belt and replace it. Scott gave the "Okay" sign and undid his buckle. He opened the weight belt and dropped it to the ocean floor. The fun began when Scott picked up his belt and placed it around his back and leaned forward. He used too much pressure to lean forward and ended up doing a somersault and dropping his weight belt. Mark and Brett started laughing again.

They had now perfected a way to breathe and laugh so water didn't fill their mouths and choke them. Scott stopped, calmed, and slowly completed the task. Skip and the two boys applauded him. Scott took a bow. The other two boys were able to complete their weight belt exercise without a hitch. The last exercise of the day was harder for each of the boys. Once everyone had completed the weight belt exercise it was time to try and take off and replace the buoyancy compensator vests. Again Skip led the way. He unzipped his vest and slowly pulled it off and set it down on the sandy bottom. He pulled his regulator from his mouth and then replaced it, blowing out first before breathing in. Skip then slowly pushed his arms through his vest, adjusted it and then zipped it up. He gave the "Okay" signal and each of the boys responded. Brett went first followed by Mark and then Scott. The boys had done well. When Scott finished his procedure Skip gave a round of applause for each boy. The Venturers then each instinctively took a bow.

Skip checked his watch and pressure gauge. It was time to head back to land. He signalled to the boys and they slowly swam back to the beach. Botany Bay was pretty shallow in most parts and the swells were mostly small, so it was easy for the boys to exit the water. The party of four regrouped and made their way back to the picnic area where Skip's assistant Rachel had been minding their gear.

"Skip, how did they go?" Rachel asked.

"The boys did well. Probably better than their compatriots before them. However, there were a couple of moments when I thought I was going to lose it. Mark replaced his mask with a fish still in it and, to top it off, Scott showed us all how to do a great somersault when replacing his weight belt. You'll have to come down next time with a video camera. It was absolutely priceless."

The boys then tried to talk their way out of what happened to them by saying they were merely performing underwater comic routines. When Rachel stopped laughing, she told Skip that Cameron had phoned and would be joining them for lunch.

"Typical. The mere smell of a barbecue and that Rover appears," Mark said.

"Yes, but he can help carry our dive gear back to the cars," Scott said with a smile.

"You know, you're simply devious, but right on the mark," Brett said.

The boys peeled off their dive gear and placed it in large plastic tubs. They towelled themselves dry and changed into shorts and T-shirts. Rachel had organised a barbecue lunch. Skip liked to put the gear away, relax with an easy lunch and talk with his students about the lesson they had just done and upcoming events.

"Skip, what's that tiny island on the tip of the other shore?" Scott asked.

"Oh, that's Cook Island. We'll be going there next week for a dive."

"Tell them about Old Blue," Cameron said as he waved to everyone and joined the group.

"Cameron, good to see you. It must be lunchtime," Skip said.

Cameron blushed as he made his way to the barbecue.

"Yes, Cameron's right. Old Blue is a giant groper that lives near the island."

"What's so special about him?" Scott asked.

"He will swim near you and start nudging you if he thinks you are friendly ... "

Cameron grabbed a sausage and placed it on a slice of bread and carried on the conversation.

"Scott, do you remember when we went to Clovelly Pool and Mike told you about feeding the gropers with sea urchin?"

"Yes."

"Well, Mike was talking about Old Blue. When he nudges you, he wants you to feed him."

"So, this is when we cut open those spongy things on the rocks and retrieve the yellow matter inside for the groper?"

"Ta-da! Right on the nose! Feed Old Blue and he remembers you. Next time you dive into the area he will seek you out."

Scott was impressed. Another adventure was waiting for him and he had only just found the key to the portal where it could begin. His dive course would pay huge dividends in fun for many years to come. Cameron caught up with the latest lesson and how the boys performed from Skip. He nearly choked on his soft drink with laughter when he heard the antics. The Rover promised Skip he would be on the next dive to assist and would bring his underwater camera. This was one piece of entertainment he didn't want to miss. The Venturers could hardly wait for the next dive and the next piece of underwater fun. It was a long time between events with a week's school yet to be completed.

Before the boys left Skip, Scott asked Cameron how the Centenary Sailing Regatta was going.

"We seem to be pretty well on track. So far we have around 100 Rovers registered to attend and more than 200 Venturers."

"Cameron, do you think we'll be going along?"

"Scott, that's up to your Unit and Mike. The Rovers are providing the activity – it's up to you whether you participate."

"Okay. I'll check with the other boys and get back to you."

"I think Mike said your boats needed re-registering. It could be a problem to find examiners to ensure the craft are ship-shape."

"Yeah. It might be solved by going diving instead anyway."

"Hang in there, Scott. Let the future unfold."

Chapter Four

Ken listened intently as the morning news broke on the radio. Police had found two men dead inside vehicles on a farm south of Sydney over the weekend. It was believed the men were affiliated with a motorcycle gang. Two people were arrested on murder charges.

The news sent goosebumps up his spine. "Please don't let it be the Eagles," Ken said to himself. "This will spark attention none of us needs." He knew of no incidents involving the Ravens. The radio announcer said Police called the murders 'an inside job' within the Eagles motorcycle gang. Ken flinched. The bodies were found after a man and his wife returned home from a shopping trip. The couple found two freshly burnt-out car wrecks on their property and investigated. Inside each of the cars, they saw the twisted and burnt remains of a human and called the Police. Four hours later Police searched a property owned by an Eagles' gang member and arrested two Eagles members, Jim Harris and Freddy O'Mara, inside. The radio report said the gangland-style murders were among the worst in the State's history.

Ken called an urgent meeting of the Ravens at his property at 7 pm that night. He knew it would take some time for all his members to clear their affairs and ride out to his property. It also allowed him time to do some research as to what was happening within the Eagles. Ken had kept in touch with a former Vietnam War Veteran who had contacts within the Eagles. Only on important issues that might stop an incident leading to bloodshed would Ken talk with his old friend. This was one of those times. It was time to open the backdoor channel between the clubs. Ken picked up his mobile phone and sent a text message to 'Macca'.

"Are the Eagle killings an inside job? Bunny."

It didn't take long for a reply.

"Not sure. Boss looking at spreading blame. Be on your toes. Macca"

Ken was now worried. Police had made no calls to either himself or his Sergeant at Arms, Damian. He was now expecting trouble. Police may have arrested two Eagles motorcycle gang members and probably had enough evidence to charge them. However, if Macca was right, then blame for the killings would be pushed on to the Ravens in some form or another by the Eagles.

The cameras watching the front approaches to Ken's property were all checked. No car or other vehicle could approach within 500 metres without showing up on the screen. Ken had also gone so far as to place sensors that could detect the weight and movement of a man, around the rear approach to his bush property. If someone over a mass of 60 kgs wandered through the bush to check out Ken's property, red lights would start flashing in his control centre and text messages sent to his phone.

Damian was the first to arrive. He always liked to be early to ensure Ken and the Raven's headquarters were protected.

"G'day mate," Damian said as he got off his 1200cc bike.

"Looks like a storm approaching."

"Hi mate. Yes. We can expect a bumpy period coming up."

Damian divested himself of his helmet, gloves and glasses and walked with Ken into the main container. The conversation was always kept at a minimum outside the container in case they were being tracked by Police with sensitive listening devices. Inside the container, an electronic hum was initiated every time the interior light switch went on. This was designed to specifically scramble any devices pointed their way. The two men walked to the rear of the container and down the special stairs to the underground bunker system.

"These Eagles killings look pretty much like someone had their hand in the till and forgot to pay up," Damian said as he took a seat on one of the lounges.

"I'm not sure who has been arrested yet but the usual messages of sympathy to the members' families have been withdrawn from the Eagles' website. If that is not a way of saying the killings were done by Eagles, I don't know what is."

Ken had sat stony-faced. He knew Damian was right.

"The real question is why do the murders in the first place and then allow two of your members to take the wrap," Ken said.

"At this stage, I can only think they were being made an example of and the Eagles leadership is sending a message to all its rank and file to toe the line."

"I've had a message from Macca who suggests the Eagles may spread the blame. The inference is we could be on the receiving end."

"Let them do it. As far as I know, we had nothing to do with these murders. There may be some bad blood between some of their members and some of ours, but not enough for this!"

The two men talked for another 40 minutes before Ken's mobile phone started going off.

"We have company. I'll see who it is …"

"Okay."

Ken retraced his steps up the stairs and out of the container. He went to his control centre and viewed the screens. Four of his members were approaching. He kept watching as the bikes made their way up the side of the property and parked outside the container. One by one the riders doffed their helmets to reveal their identities. Ken recognised Tim, Trevor, Robert, and Jim. They were the nucleus of the club and had helped form it some five years ago. He went out to meet them.

"Hi guys. Thanks for coming."

A round of 'G'day mate' was heard as each biker said hello and walked forward to shake hands with Ken.

"Damian is already here and organising the first round of drinks."

"What a mate … always looking after us," Trevor said.

"That's why we made him Sergeant at Arms," Robert said.

The five men went into the container past the spare parts and down the stairs into the clubhouse bunker system.

"Damo, I could smell that first beer mate. Oh, by the way, how are you?" Jim asked with a flourish.

The other bikies laughed as they shook hands with their Sergeant at Arms and reached into the fridge to retrieve a beer. The sound of the tin tabs being pulled from cans and the effervescent beers rang out in the bunker. Within 30 minutes the remaining members had arrived, made their way downstairs and opened their beers. Ken ensured the doors to the container were shut by activating a remote control.

Damian took the floor as the group's Sergeant At Arms and updated everyone with the latest information regarding the Eagles. He was not afraid of a stoush but was worried about how the Police could react towards them if the Eagles started a misinformation campaign. Damian was a good man to be around if a fight broke out. He was not afraid of anyone, which sometimes riled his other club members. Whereas most of the Ravens would exercise restraint when dealing with difficult situations, Damian would barge ahead and to hell with the consequences.

"Virtually all we know so far is what has been broadcast on the news," Damian said.

"Two Eagles members were found dead in burnt-out cars on a property. Two of their club members have been arrested and charged with murder. Someone called Freddy O'Mara and Jim Harris. This almost sounds cut and dry. Except, Ken received other information that alarmed us both. Ken … "

"Thanks, Damo," Ken said as he stood up. He paused and looked at each of his club members in turn.

"I have a mate who knows some of the Eagle boys and he's told me Rick Lane could be looking at spreading the blame for the murders. This would mean he's trying to not only send a message inside his club but also have an excuse to bring on a war with us."

"What's the point?" Jim asked.

"He kills two birds with one stone. Err, sorry for the pun. Lane not only sends a message to his members to shape up over whatever issue started all this but also toughens them up by bringing on a war with us."

Tim thought it was time to test his research. He outlaid his plans for a new clubhouse at Cook Island in Botany Bay as a backup where a full-on war could be raged with reduced or little effect against the Ravens.

"Mate, this would be a pretty drastic move if we go to Cook Island," Robert said as he opened his third beer.

"From the sounds of it, we'd be stuck like rats on an island with no escape if the wallopers came in guns blazing to stop the Eagles and us having some fun."

Tim stood his ground. "No, we would have a fantastic escape route. On the point side of the island is a small wharf and we could anchor a boat with a floating barge-type device behind it. If the tide ever turned against us we'd only have to ride onto the island, onto the wharf and make a water escape."

He surveyed the other club members who seemed to be mulling over what he had just said. "Ken and the rest of us have invested a lot of money into this place to make it invisible and secure. What I am proposing now is to keep this place as a backup and move to Cook Island until the Eagles' issue blows over."

Trevor had been silent long enough. He put his right hand up in a gesture to quieten Tim and took the floor.

"Mate, what you have done as far as research goes is commendable. Lucky you work for the National Parks people. I think we should make three moves. The first is to talk to anyone we know who can give us an inside reading of what the Eagles are up to.

"Second, we start grouping together more often and in numbers so we can't be easily picked off. Lastly, Tim and Damian should check out Cook Island. Maybe take a few photos and show us what is there and the sorts of approaches, defences, and vantage points. I'd certainly want to know whether we could escape the place if it all turns to the proverbial with cops crawling all over the place."

The rest of the Ravens agreed. Tim and Damian said they would check out Cook Island the following weekend. The meeting lasted a couple of hours before the Ravens made their way out of the bunker and into the night air for their respective rides home.

Chapter Five

U nbeknown to the Ravens, Rick Lane had also called a
meeting of his members. The Eagles' clubhouse was set
in a former industrial estate. It had a large tin fence around the
whole perimeter and the main clubhouse was a former small
warehouse. There was enough parking inside the clubhouse
walls for around 150 bikes – not that the Eagles would ever
have that many members. They were lucky to have around
15 full-time members and a series of hangers-on. Police had
raided the clubhouse several times over the years and arrested
a couple of Eagles' members who were caught making illicit
drugs ready to sell on the open market. Since then, the Eagles
had fortified their gates and added cameras to help secure their
compound.

The Police, on the other hand, had complained to the State
Premier of needing armoured vehicles, similar to the Army,
to help with crowd control. The complaints came close on
the heels of two race riots in Sydney. One at an inner-city
suburb involving local indigenous people and the second, a
much larger fracas between other ethnic groups at a beach.
The Premier acquiesced and bought one vehicle. It was shaped
similar to the Australian Light Armoured Vehicle or ASLAV
used by the Australian Army in its overseas deployments. It

could be fitted with a huge bulbar to allow it to forcibly enter virtually any building in the State. The Eagles were aware of the Police acquisition but had not done anything to bolster their clubhouse defences to try and thwart it.

Rick Lane told his members it looked like the two dead Eagles had been set up by the Ravens. He showed photos of Ravens members Trevor, Damian and Tim leaving Theos bar in Kings Cross after they had beaten up the security guards and stolen their expected standover money.

"We think these three have turned renegade within the Ravens and are trying to shift the blame on their dwindling standover racket and drugs money up at Kings Cross," Rick said. "Our blokes, Gordo and Johnno, had been doing the rounds of the shopkeepers and businesses when they went missing.

"Next thing I know, their bodies were found in a couple of burnt-out cars and the cops are raiding Jimbo's and Freddy's places with some sort of story they found evidence at the scene they did the other boys in."

A pin could have been heard to drop on the floor of the meeting room. The Eagles were keen to know what had happened. There hadn't been a death in their 'family' for some time. Not only had there been two deaths, but two of their members were in custody and war was looming with the Ravens. The Eagles hotly debated the issues with each other as to why four of their members were no longer around. Copious amounts of alcohol were drunk and some illicit cigarettes were smoked as the bikies consoled each other. Rick and his Sergeant at Arms, Benny, went to check their bikes.

"It seems our weakest links have now met their fates," Rick said as he crouched down to check the drive shaft of Benny's motorcycle. Benny crouched down with him and pointed at parts of his bike in a mock gesture in case anyone was watching the pair.

"Yes. The two we suspected of ripping the Eagles off by pocketing the standover money up at Kings Cross met a fiery end, one could say. The other two … well, let's say there is some pretty strong evidence they were trying to branch out on their own with drug making and selling their drugs to our clients. They'll have a hard time getting out of the murder charges. Either way, they are dead meat."

"Yes. In gaol, members of other gangs won't have a bar of them and may even try and rearrange their appearances," Rick said.

"If they get bail, the Eagles may want to rearrange their bodies for breaking our code and setting up their own business. A good lesson to anyone else."

The two men started laughing and stood up.

"Now we best plan the funerals of our dear departed comrades," Rick said.

"Yes, we need some sort of demonstration that we miss them. I'll start the planning and get back to you soon. It will be a while before the coroner releases the bodies."

The men made their way back into the alcoholic haze of their main meeting room and re-joined the other Eagles. They had to ensure their members were kept on the side, kept in line and kept abreast of not starting any businesses without the Eagles' approval.

It didn't take long. Within 48 hours of the two dead Eagles' bodies being found, motorcycle riders were seen riding near Ken's property. Video footage showed a couple of riders driving around the Ravens' meeting area and stopping every so often to discuss things. When a couple of Ravens members rode to the property, the Eagles took off.

The following night, Ken's property was hit by a couple of people leaning out of cars without number plates and throwing Molotov cocktails. The deadly liquid ignited quickly when the bottles it was contained in, smashed on Ken's front gate and grassland. The burning cloth wicks in the neck of the bottles ensured instant ignition. Several rifle shots had also been fired at the main building on the property. The Ravens were incensed. They were being targeted for murders they had not committed. They were also being blamed for pinning the murders on two other Eagle members.

Police had become quite edgy over the brewing brouhaha. Commissioner Rex Small knew the motorcycle gangs had strong allegiances to each other and was worried an open war could erupt on the streets of Sydney. He called a meeting with his two Deputy Commissioners and Commander of the Motorcycle Gang Squad, Detective Superintendent Paul McPherson.

The Commissioner was apprised of the latest incidents involving the attacks on the Ravens and the investigation into the two murders of the Eagles members.

"No doubt there will be a large funeral somewhere and bikie groups from around Australia may attend," the Commissioner said. "We have to ensure we are more than prepared for any eventuality and I want a crackdown on all bikie members that have anything to do with the funeral and burial services."

The Commissioner's directive had also been relayed to the State Premier to alert him of possible public safety issues and how the Police were preparing for them. Four days after the two Eagles' bodies had been found in burnt-out cars, the Coroner released the bodies for burial. The Coroner's move set in motion a series of events that consumed the news media.

The funerals of Gordon Bennett aged 31 and John Roberts aged 32, were held together in St Catherine's Church near the Eagles' clubhouse. Police security at the Church and along the route to the cemetery was unrivalled. It would have equalled that of a Prime Ministerial visit. More than 250 uniformed Police were deployed to quell any likely disturbance at the service and burial and to ensure any wakes held afterwards were peaceful. The Police had started taking up positions the night before the funerals at every vantage point they could. They wanted to ensure there were no issues with rival motorcycle gangs that could spill over into the public arena.

The Police Commissioner issued a warning through the Media to all motorcycle groups attending the funeral that any breach of the law would be dealt with swiftly. Around 120 motorcycle riders joined the family members of the two murdered bikers. The funeral procession was spread for hundreds of metres as the bike riders rode ahead of the corteges and cars containing family members of the deceased.

Tensions rose when Police pulled down a couple of banners on overhead pedestrian bridges along the route to the cemetery, farewelling the murdered bike riders. Calm was restored at the cemetery when Eagles' Sergeant at Arms, Benny, spoke with senior police. A truce was agreed to between the bike riders and the Police and orderly burial services and dispersal of riders afterwards took place.

Detective Superintendent McPherson told the Media no charges had been laid throughout the funerals. A wake for both Eagles was held at the Eagles' clubhouse with around 90 riders from around the country attending. All bikes were ridden inside the fenced-off former industrial estate and parked to stop unwanted police attention. During the all-night drinking session, several plots against the Ravens were hatched. The Eagles' numbers would temporarily swell for the next few weeks while the drug making, drug selling, racketeering and prostitution services would be bolstered. This was to ensure a tight squeeze was placed on the Ravens to force them out of their business roles.

"Rick, this is the best response we could have asked for," Benny said as he reached for another beer.

"We seem to have sold the idea well that it was time to crack down on anyone who decided to keep money from our operations for themselves. Also, it is time the Ravens were forced out of business and run out of town. The bonus is the loan of extra biker muscle, minus their share, for our business arms."

Rick looked at Benny and then moved closer to him.

"So far, so good. Things are working for us in two ways.

"Firstly, the boys' murders have given the rest of our members something to think about when trying to keep the money for themselves. No doubt they'll watch the Court cases of Jimbo and Freddy closely.

"Secondly, we have to ensure there is no room for the Ravens to work in any area where we have business arms. This will allow us to expand all our enterprises."

"You know this will start a war with the Ravens?"

"Yes. But the resultant publicity will alert the other clubs we are THE force to be reckoned with in Sydney. We'll need to call a full meeting of our Chapter in a couple of days' time to sort the details and prepare ourselves."

"Okay boss. Best we get back to the drinking before it all goes."

The men re-joined the other bikies at the wake.

Chapter Six

It was a perfect day for a dive. Hardly a cloud in the sky and calm waters. The viz or vision underwater was fantastic. This meant any diver could see for quite a few metres underwater with good clarity.

"Scott, did you bring your first aid kit? Cameron asked as he picked up the Venturer from his home.

"Yes."

"What about your box of spare parts for your fins, mask etc?"

"That, I didn't think of. I'll be right back," Scott said as he darted back inside his home to retrieve his container of spare parts. The spares were needed in case little things like the back strap on your fins, the strap of your mask or O-rings from your dive tank suddenly broke. They saved a dive cancellation or a long haul to a dive shop for a small part worth a few cents to help you enjoy your dive.

Scott returned with his plastic-trayed toolbox and got into the rear of Cameron's car with Brett. Mark was already in the passenger front seat.

"Mike rang me today and will be joining us for a dive," Cameron said.

"What about Skip taking us," Mark asked.

"He can't make it today. Mike is a dive master too, so no probs. He'll make up the team numbers so we can more easily pair off when we start exploring and go looking for Old Blue."

"Yeah," Scott said.

"I'm looking forward to feeding this fish and sharing his world."

"Just be careful when he comes near you. We don't want to frighten him off. He's been around for a long time," Cameron said.

"I aim to befriend him, not hurt him," Scott said. "I want to learn from Old Blue and let him know he has another friend. Maybe, he can share an adventure with us. That would be interesting."

The Venturers laughed among themselves as they spoke about playing tag with Old Blue or getting him to show them some underwater treasure. The boys were envisaging a Disney movie in the making. Cameron parked his car in a car park overlooking a giant grassy rock island with large concrete bunker-style buildings. A wooden bridge was suspended between the mainland below the car park and the rocky island.

"There she is boys. Cook Island," Cameron said.

"We'll be diving on the western or left-hand side and following the island about halfway around."

Scott became excited. The island had been a military fort and may still have cannon around somewhere. Any wonder Mike was keen to dive today, he thought.

"So how deep is it?" Mark asked.

"It starts around a metre and goes to about 20 metres on the other side of the island," Cameron said.

"If you look to your right on top of the grassy hill there's an old column that looks like a giant chess piece ..."

"Was there a castle built here too?" Brett asked.

"This is all wrong. Australia never had castles ... we're too young."

"Whoa! The big rock area is Cook Island and was used by the Government as a fort in the 1800s," Cameron said.

"Later it was used by Customs to stop drug runners and others bringing illicit material into the country. Finally, it was used as a repatriation hospital for war veterans I think before the place started to have problems with its structural integrity. Now, it's a great place to hold weddings and other functions."

The boys got out of the car and started looking around. Scott looked at Cook Island and then at the sandstone column that resembled the castle chess piece.

"I'll lay odds it was some sort of observation tower," Scott said as he pointed to the giant chess piece. "Hey, get a look at Cook Island. Wow."

Cameron smiled as he watched the expressions on the faces of each of the Venturers.

"Not a bad piece of real estate – just a pity about the dodgy building work," Cameron said. "Then again, if it closes down, it would be a terrific place to play war games. What do you think Mike?"

"I'm up for a good war gaming water pistol fight any time."

Scott broke out in a smile. His Venturer Unit loved playing games of stalking each other in bushland and capturing their opponents. Weapons of choice were huge water pistols painted in camouflage colours or wrapped in hessian.

"I'll remember you said that Mike. Especially next time I have my water pistol in hand."

"Nice one Scott."

Mike and the Venturers changed into their diving gear beside their cars. They walked down a winding bitumen road to the wooden footbridge leading to Cook Island. The group then descended a set of stairs to the rock ledge below and the edge of the water. They checked each other's gear to ensure all was correctly positioned, turned on and ready to go. The group went in pairs to the water's edge. They then performed the diver's ritual of steadying their mate while he put his fins over his rubber booty shoes. This helped save the diver putting on the fins from falling over or being knocked off their feet by waves. Eventually, the pairs of divers made their way into the water channel and blew air into their buoyancy compensator vests to keep them afloat.

"Work to the left and follow the rock wall around the island," Cameron said. "Keep an eye out for Old Blue and alert the rest of us if you see him."

Scott turned to Brett and said he hoped the groper was around today and not feeding off other divers. Brett agreed and the pair started swimming out towards the island. Once the group had crossed the channel between the mainland and the island Mike gave the diver's signal asking if all was okay. One by one the group placed their right hands on their heads in an arc to signal they were okay. Mike signalled for the group to descend and one by one they lifted their vest lines upright, pushed their purge valves and squeezed their vests to push the air out. Each then started sinking towards the sandy bottom.

One by one each of the groups added air to their vests or squeezed more out to adjust their diving plane and buoyancy.

Finally, Mike knelt at the bottom and signalled for the group to join him. One by one the Venturers and Cameron also knelt to form a circle around Mike. The Venturer Leader then placed his right thumb and index fingers together to form the underwater 'okay' sign. In unison, the group did the same. Mike then opened his right hand and pointed forward and started swimming. The boys and Cameron automatically paired off and swam in a line around the island base. The look on the boy's faces through their masks said it all. Each was excited and awed by the beautiful rock colours and fish. Occasionally pairs of divers would stop and investigate beautiful fish or rock coral.

Scott was absorbed in the antics of an octopus he had seen dart in front of him towards a rock crevice. He failed to notice a dark shadow approaching his left shoulder. When Old Blue nudged Scott the youth turned his head in shock and then started swimming backwards in a move to escape the monster from the deep. Cameron and Mike laughed as they watched their young charge deal with his first encounter with Old Blue. Scott was initially taken aback when the groper nudged him. He had been too focused on the octopus to keep a wider awareness of his surroundings. When he realised the fish was trying to make friends, a calm came over him and he reached out slowly to see if the fish would nibble his fingers. Old Blue slowly swam towards the rear of Scott and nudged his tank. Scott looked to Mike and his leader pointed to his knife and the spongy sea urchin on the seabed.

"Okay, old man, it's feeding time," Scott said in his mind.

He slowly pulled out his knife and knelt on the sea floor. The youth then scraped at the base of a sea urchin and lifted it from its rocky bed. He carefully cut into it to reveal the soft yellow flesh of the centre and took it in his left hand. Old Blue came closer and eyed Scott cautiously. Scott casually opened his hand and the groper swam to him. The fish ate the yellow flesh in seconds and looked at Scott in a manner that said he wanted more.

Mark picked up on what Scott had done and opened his sea urchin. Within seconds, Old Blue had a new friend. In turn, each of the other divers did the same until they had all fed the big fish. Mike then signalled it was time to move on and further explore the rock wall before returning to the start point. The group kept swimming and the ocean floor seemed to drop away further and further. Scott checked his depth gauge and saw he was around 20 metres under the ocean. He looked up. The sky was somewhere upwards where his air bubbles seemed to be racing. The view upwards was fascinating in itself as it went from the light around him to a few various shades of grey and blue and then dim white. Brett tapped Scott on the shoulder, and he turned quickly to see what the problem was now.

Brett pointed to some odd shapes on the ground near an outlet pipe at the base of the rock wall. Scott went to investigate but was held back by his mate. Brett then pointed to Scott and brought both his hands up in front of him in a sign to stay put. He then pointed to the shapes again, closed his hands and keeping the bottom of his palms together, opened and closed his hands. The action looked like he was signalling there was a crocodile below. There wasn't. The crocs don't live so far south in Australia. Brett then swam to Mike and Cameron and tapped them on their shoulders. He then pointed to where Scott was floating and motioned for them to follow. The pair slowly kicked their way towards Scott and then looked at Brett. The boy pointed to a couple of moving shapes on the ocean floor and the group started laughing. Brett started to swim towards the shapes when Mike darted in front of him and stopped him. Mike then slowly swam around the shapes and went over to Scott. He motioned for Scott to give him his underwater camera. Scott undid his zippered pocket and extracted his camera and gave it to Mike.

Slowly, Mike swam around the moving shapes and took photos. He then signalled to the group of Venturers to return to the beginning of the dive. The boys and Cameron reformed in pairs and swam along the rock wall and slowly made their way to the surface, taking in all the sights of coral, coloured rocks and small schools of fish in all shapes and sizes. Mike stopped the group. He closed his right hand and extended his thumb and waved his hand up and down. The boys knew this was the end of the dive and signalled back okay. Each then slowly surfaced with their partner.

"What the hell were those shapes, Mike?" Brett asked hurriedly.

"This is not a sex education lecture but what we saw were two wobbegongs mating. They are not dangerous to us, but given what they were doing, they probably didn't want to be interrupted."

Each of the boys started laughing as they realised what

Mike was saying. They were keen to discuss the find and Mike knew they would be bursting with questions. They inflated their vests again and swam back to shore. The ritual of doffing their fins so they could walk on the rocks played out slowly as each of the pairs of divers was buffeted slightly by onshore waves.

Mike grouped the Venturers in a tight circle around him. "What did you think of Old Blue and his little wobbegong friends?"

"It was fantastic to feed Old Blue and have him eat out of your hand. I never thought it was possible," Brett said.

Scott was laughing. "You know, when you closed your hands and started opening and closing them together, I thought you were pointing to some crocodiles. I started getting a bit worried. Then I realised they don't like the cold water down here. Phew."

The group gathered their gear and walked back to the cars to get changed. A row of motorcycles was near the lone sandstone sentry point with a group of leather-clad bikers all talking loudly. The boys started getting changed and putting their dive gear away in the cars when Scott sidled up to Mike.

"An interesting group of people behind us?"

"Yes. Do you realise the cost of their bikes can sometimes be the cost of a car or more?"

"No. I would have thought the bikes would cost less because they only have two wheels and there are a lot less moving parts."

"Good try, Scott. We should get some bikers over to the hall one night so they can tell us about their lifestyles and bikes. It would be good to know more about them from their side, not just what you read in the papers."

"You know that was the first time I have ever seen a sea horse in the wild," Mark said.

Brett started laughing. "You reckon that was great, Scott and I chased an octopus down into a crevice and saw what looked like an eel hiding."

Scott gave him a hand to lift a dive bucket with the boys' regulators into Mike's car boot. He warily eyed the bikers as they stood next to their road machines and drank cans of beer. An eerie feeling came over him.

"I reckon this has got to be one of the best adventures we've had so far," Scott said. "Clovelly pool was awesome in the storm, but feeding Old Blue and chasing schools of fish and an octopus is pretty high on my list of delights."

Cameron had fully changed out of his dive gear and re-joined the Venturers to give them a hand with the equipment.

"So mate, this is better than being locked in lighthouses or rescuing people in canyons or from trees, eh?"

Scott steeled himself. "Cameron, I was forced into situations I didn't want to be in and did the best I could to get out of them. Here, diving is my choice and I can do it at my pace. It has to rate as excellent. Yes, it has an element of danger. But what a buzz going into the world of fish and seeing how they play and do business. Now, I'm really looking forward to doing some more."

Cameron looked concerned after he viewed the bikers drinking nearby. He wanted to get the boys out of the area as soon as practicable yet still look quite normal with his processes. The Rover was feeling the Venturers were indirectly being scrutinised by the bikers and he wanted to get the boys out of any potential harm's way. It took a few more minutes before the group was ready to go.

"Cam, I'll meet you at the dive shop," Mike said.

"Okay, Mike. See you there."

The group got into their cars and headed back to Skip's dive shop where they had obtained the equipment. Within minutes of arriving at the shop, the boys were emptying the cars of dive equipment and taking it to the rear of the shop. A production line was set up where the boys would wash or hose down the equipment and then hang it up to dry. While this was taking place, Skip had started a barbecue and was cooking sausages so the boys could rid themselves of the saltwater taste left in their mouths from diving.

"I reckon they were pretty expensive bikes," Mark said as he hosed down his dive suit.

"Imagine how fast they would go on a long straight stretch. What a thrill that would be," Brett chipped in.

Scott smiled. "There's no way I'd ever buy a bike. I guess I just love the thought of four wheels under me and lots of metal forming a barrier between me and whatever is in front of me."

The boys became engrossed in their pontifications and production line.

"Come on you lot, get a move on," Mike said as he walked back into the rear of the shop to check on the boys.

"I know, it's time for a sausage sandwich, right?" Cameron asked. He couldn't help with a joke at Mike's expense.

The Venturer Leader surveyed the scene. The boys had

hosed down and rinsed the equipment. All the wetsuits and buoyancy vests were hanging up to dry and the various air tanks were in the rear of the shop ready to be re-filled. A good feeling came over him. The boys were good at working as a team. It was a shame he thought that they had to move on to Rovers when they reached 18 as they were working so well together.

Then again, other adventures waited for them at another level.

Chapter Seven

Tim was becoming restless. He had organised for a small boat to drop off a plastic box containing 10 rifles and a second box with 500 5.56 mm rounds of ammunition in a few weeks. The weapons and ammunition were enough for a small firefight. Tim was first on the scene at the sentry tower opposite Cook Island and waited for some other Ravens to arrive. Damian and Trevor soon joined him along with Rod. The four had surveyed the scene and started drinking cans of beer they had stashed in their bike's pannier bags with layers of crystallised ice in small bubble packages – the same as athletes use when they are injured on the field. The bikers walked to the edge of the mainland and surveyed the scene. No boats in sight, several people milling, playing and walking around the edge of the rocky shores. No problems so far.

They had watched earlier as the Venturers made their way to the cars, got changed and packed their gear away. It didn't take the boys long to be ready for the transport back to the dive shop. The two groups of males couldn't have been more different in their lifestyles, yet each had a strong allegiance to their respective group.

Tim described the inside of Cook Island to the other three and explained how it could be set up as an alternate headquarters for the Ravens.

"If Ken won't commit to a full-time headquarters, we can

at least use this place while we work out how to rid ourselves of the Eagles, once and for all," he said.

Rod sipped his beer and pointed to the rocky island fortress. "If we take over the place, won't it be just too easy for the Eagles to cut the approach to the island and have us locked in?"

"That would be their thinking. However, we have some extra pieces at play. The first is a boat tied to a jetty at the side of the fort in case we get blocked in. The second is a chess piece."

Tim pointed to the lone sentry tower and described how a couple of Raven members could install themselves on top and act as both lookouts and the first line of defence.

"There is only one road into this place, and it forms a loop in front of the old museum, café, graveyard and a bunch of shops," Tim said. "If we were to sucker the Eagles into coming down the loop road, we could block their exit and have them trapped in the open.

"We would have the fort for our main thrust, the sentry tower as a first backup and the boat as our secondary escape. We also need a couple of trucks to block the road, so the Eagles are bottled up."

Damian was thinking it through. "It could work. It could be a very effective area to fight if there are no civilians here to get in the way ... and there is a final water escape if required."

Trevor was more pensive. "Are you sure you will have a boat at the jetty waiting for us. ... just in case the cops come in and the Eagles get the better of us?"

Tim took them through the scenario once more of organising

for a boat large enough to take the Ravens members away at a good speed. He then spoke about luring the Eagles into a group stoush around the loop road. Police would be blocked from entering the road once the Eagles were bottled up and engaged. The rest would be a turkey shoot. The only entrances to the area would be by water or air. Police were not equipped with canon on their boats or aircraft – only Defence and Customs. However, as the gang fight would be a civil affair, only the Police would be involved.

"The piece in this chess game would be our special exit strategy," Tim said. "I spoke to Ken and together we came up with a boat and special flat bottom pontoon with side rails. The boat and pontoon will be berthed at the wharf at the point on the other side of the fort. If it all turns to the proverbial, we ride along the carriageway, around the fort and onto the pontoon. The Eagles couldn't follow us and we make our way into Botany Bay and a quick escape, leaving our rivals at the mercy of the cops."

"Mate, you really need to sell this to a full meeting of the Ravens, so you get maximum support," Damian said.

"Once we start this firefight with the Eagles there will be no stopping until they are either wiped out or they give up. Our aim isn't necessarily to kill them, but put them into a position where they know we are boss and for them to leave our protected shops alone."

Rod still wasn't quite sold on the idea of the biker's last stand. "How do we handle anyone getting shot or injured? You want the roads blocked so no ambulances can get in. If anyone gets shot or wounded pretty bad, they'll end up dying here."

Tim looked at Rod and then the other Ravens with him. "Our aim is not to murder the Eagles. However, if they do get wounded in our little fight, so be it."

"I'm not trying to be a wet blanket here Tim. What if we get hit too? A lot of the Eagles carry sawn-off shotguns in their panniers too."

"Mate, you know the beauty of our weapons. We can fire them from long distances with pretty good accuracy. The cut-down shotguns are only effective for a few metres in front of the firer. We'll have the advantage. Anyway, if worse comes to worst and we are injured, we can use the boat and pontoon positioned at the point to get out of here."

The group agreed. They walked to the edge of the mainland to watch night fall and then did a walk around the loop road working out how they would each see the impending battle take place and the pros and cons of where they would need to be positioned and with what firearms. Tim's weapons would be dropped off within a fortnight on the left-hand side of Cook Island, near an outlet pipe. He planned to take the weapons into the island at night through the pipes and prepare them for battle. The new weapons would still have loads of grease on them and would need to be thoroughly cleaned and oiled before they could be used. A night shoot from the other side of Cook Island would cap off the Ravens' training and allow them to sight their weapons. Ken's cousin would supply a boat and pontoon for the firefight. Tim was happy.

Tim had secured a copy of the master keys to the security gates on Cook Island, the interior chambers and doors. By nightfall, nearly all the people milling around the water's edge had left. The Ravens quietly walked across the wooden bridge built to carry single horse-drawn carriages in an era long gone. It was a time when roads were called carriageways as carriages were the main mode of transport. The group made their way into the old fortress. Security lights had been left on which made the group's passage through the military maze easier.

"This place is awesome," Damian said as he looked at the well-polished floors. "This must have been a great place to recuperate as an injured soldier. It's a stark contrast to the sorts of hospitals we have today for everyone, regardless if you are a soldier or not."

The others agreed. Tim took the group through the rooms used as wards, the operating theatre and finally down to the old magazine-holding areas where ammunition was held for the main guns on the island.

"What's the pool for?" Trevor asked.

"This is the entrance to the outlet pipe leading to the ocean," Tim said. "When the rifles and ammo are dropped off we'll have to swim through this rectangular hole and out along the pipe. The good thing is, no one will see the weapons and ammo dropped off and no one will see us pick them up. This way, our little booty will be a surprise to any prying eyes."

Rod started laughing. "Are you trying to tell me you can hold your breath that long you can just swim out through the pipes, retrieve the rifles and haul them back in one breath? I don't think so!"

"No, you goose. We'll have to use scuba gear to go and get them. I've done diving on a holiday before and so has Damian. We'll go and get the bang sticks."

"Thank you. That detail was worrying me. I don't mind facing off with the Eagles as this will be our turf. However, out there, through the pipes and in the ocean … that's a whole different story. What about using Ken's boat and pontoon? Wouldn't that make it easier?"

"No, as the boat will only be available for our emergency exit. In other words, only on the day of the fight."

The Ravens walked around the pool and then made their way up a set of crumbling concrete stairs to an outside viewing platform.

"Watch your step. The edge line of the stairs could give way at any time," Tim said. "We don't need anyone hurt here, do we?"

The view across Botany Bay was fantastic. Tiny lights from factories and houses across the bay gave an eerie feel of childhood charm. In another era, the Ravens would have been told to look at the fairy lights by their parents and see if any of the lights turned into fireflies. The vast open water added a touch of serenity. Way out in the ocean, just below the horizon, a large ship laden with stacks of containers slowly plied its way south. The bikers stood mesmerised for a few minutes as they took in the view.

"Any wonder the National Parks have kept this place open for weddings so long," Damian said. "A lot of people would pay handsomely for a view like this on their special day."

Tim took the group back through the island fortress and out to the wooden bridge. He quietly locked the gates behind them before they strode back along the carriageway leading to the mainland.

"Well gents, what do you think?" Tim asked as he scanned each of the Ravens' faces.

"I think we have a plan," Damian said as he broke out into a sinister grin.

Rod raised his shoulders in a "don't know" fashion and then said the plan had great merits but may need tweaking. Trevor readily smiled and said he was raring to go. The group made their way back to their bikes and put their helmets on. They had agreed to meet within a few days to shore up the support of the rest of the Ravens and confirm their plans. The sounds of the bikes sparking into life echoed around the area. Black helmets, black boots and black leather jackets made it pretty impossible to determine who was who. Only the variety of the motorcycles themselves gave away the identity of the riders.

Chapter Eight

It was 6.58 pm and Mandy and the rest of the Ranger Guides were getting ready for the opening ceremony.

Two of the Rangers had brought the flags and flag holder out from the cupboard and placed them at the front of the hall in preparation for the opening. Miss Anne Hinchley, or *Rosie*, as she liked to be called in Guiding, had finally cut away from talking to some of the girls' parents and made her way to the front of the hall. She was impressed. Mandy and Liane had organised the Rangers well.

There must be something they are after, she thought.

She quietly walked to the flags and stood in front. Rosie stood in the 'at ease' position. She then called the Unit to 'attention'. The Rangers all stood boldly upright with hands by their sides. Rosie scanned the Unit and asked for the 'Colour party' to fall out. Mandy, Liane and a third Ranger Guide stepped forward to do the 'colours'.

Mandy was to handle the flag and the other two girls were her flag escorts. The Rangers retrieved the flag and marched through the horseshoe formation. The Unit saluted the flag as the colour party passed them. The three Rangers stopped in front of the flag stand. Mandy stepped forward and placed the flag in the stand. She stepped back into the colour party and gave the command 'Colour party salute the flag.' The three girls smartly saluted the flag. Mandy then called out 'Colour party about turn'. The girls marched back to the place at the base of the horseshoe.

Rosie brought the girls to the at ease position and explained the night's program. She then brought the girls to the attention position and told them to 'fall out', a command signifying to the girls to take one step forward and two steps back before moving away to go to their bags and get changed, ready for the night's activities.

"Okay girls, I need some back-up here," Mandy said as she changed from her crisply ironed white blouse to a T-shirt.

"We're with you Mandy," Liane and Rebecca said.

"Okay, let's make it happen," Mandy replied.

The Rangers played a fast ball game and then sat down to discuss the upcoming term program. A groundswell of support was now emerging for newer and more adventurous activities. Mandy took the lead.

"Rosie, a couple of us have some suggestions for activities for the next month."

"Great. Rebecca, how about you start writing them on the whiteboard?"

"Okay."

Mandy took a deep breath. "You remember when we were at the Clovelly Surf Club for the fundraising event and we saw those people going snorkelling? Can we do the same?" The other girls joined in with a resounding chorus of 'great idea', 'sounds fine by me'.

"Whoa! Those idiots were snorkelling at night in a storm

and could have been swept out to sea. There's no way we're going to do the same."

"Rosie, I spoke with kids at school and they told me those 'idiots' were Venturers."

"I rest my case!"

"They had glow sticks on their snorkels for safety and a Rover walking on the outside of the pool acting as a safety officer, so no one went more than halfway along the pool to the rock wall at the ocean.

"Couldn't we do the same please?" We must have some Rover equivalents from Guides or leaders that could help us?"

"There is no way you'll ever get me in the water at night, glow sticks or not," Rosie said as she started to redden in the face.

"It is just too dangerous. On face value, I can't see Chegs, approving the activity either. As far as Guide equivalents for the Rovers, we don't have too many around our area. Any other ideas?"

"Rosie, before you dismiss it out of hand, I want to let you know I have spoken with some girls at school who are sisters of the boys we saw at Clovelly.

"They told us the boys would be keen to have a combined activity like night, or even twilight snorkelling when there's more light."

"Do the Venturers come from Clovelly?"

"No. They're from 1st Hurstville – just up the road from us."

Liane joined in a matter of factly. "These are the boys who were captured by the Russian drug mafia up at Myall Lakes and were in the news.

"Don't you remember? One of the boys, Scott Morrow, escaped from an old convict jail the Unit was locked in, climbed a lighthouse and then turned it into a weapon to help capture the Mafia."

Rosie was taken aback by her Ranger's latest input. "So, these are the Venturers who grabbed world headlines with the arrest of the Russians and their mother ship?"

"Yes and no," Liane continued. "They helped capture some Russians, but Defence and Customs got the mother ship. These are also the same Venturers who helped set up the National Rover Emergency Rescue Service we've all heard about."

Mandy couldn't contain herself either and quickly jumped back into the conversation. "Scott was the Venturer who not only set up the Rover Emergency Rescue Service but helped rescue two people on a canyoning trip shortly afterwards in the Blue Mountains."

"Well, I'd like to meet these Venturers. They sound like they have been through hell and back and undergone a huge lot of experience in the meantime," Rosie said.

"They're a bit shy and don't really talk about their exploits," Mandy said. "They just kept on Venturing after their various ordeals. Now they are keen to meet up with our Ranger Unit and combine some activities with us."

Rosie was backed into a corner. She had reached middle age and didn't want to lead the more adventurous activities anymore. What made matters worse was that she had no junior leader to assist, and the current crop of teenage girls was more like tom-boys who craved outdoor adventurous activities.

"Nothing is impossible. I can talk with Chegs about the

snorkelling. If you get the Venturers leader's phone number and details, I'll ring him and see what we can arrange," Rosie said with a smile.

"The first activity we have to organise is for a going on or investiture ceremony for Claudia in a fortnight. She'll be joining us from Guides."

"How about we take her to Cook Island where we can have a picnic lunch on the grassy common near the old sandstone observation tower?" Rebecca asked.

"Good idea. What else would you do there?" Rosie asked, waiting for the trap to be sprung.

Mandy came in almost on cue. "We could hold the ceremony on the common and then visit the museum there and check out Cook Island and the nearby beaches."

Rosie had smelled a rat but agreed with the idea. At least the girls hadn't said they wanted to go snorkelling or swimming.

"The museum there is dedicated to the French who arrived a short time after Captain James Cook did in 1770," Mandy said.

"The priest who was with the French died in the area and is buried in a special grave next to the museum."

Rosie looked surprised. "You seem to have it all sorted. We'll need to work out timings and then get the next few weeks down as well."

Mandy and Liane looked at each other and smiled. Mission accomplished. They had wanted to check out Cook Island for a possible guided tour with the Venturers they had seen at Clovelly Pool. They knew through their classmates at school the boys were planning a dive at Cook Island shortly and wanted to meet them in daylight. Both girls started sending mobile phone text messages to their friends to check when the Venturers were going diving.

Rosie moved on to talk about an upcoming sleepover at the zoo to raise money for the homeless.

"YES!" Mandy said out loud, forgetting she was still in a meeting.

Her school friend had sent her a message saying her brother and his Venturer Unit had set the date of diving at Cook Island for Saturday fortnight. All was on track for meeting the boys and getting some ideas for adventurous activities.

Rosie frowned and looked at Mandy. "Put your mobile phone away! This is a Ranger Guide meeting, not a texting session."

"Sorry, Rosie!"

Mandy managed to set Saturday fortnight as the going-on ceremony date with Rosie. She then organised with the rest of the Unit details of the zoo sleep-out and a couple of more activities. Liane had been busy confirming details with her classmates of their brothers' contact details.

This would be a day to remember for all the Ranger Guides.

Chapter Nine

Detective Superintendent Paul McPherson was working hard, deep in the bowels of the Police Headquarters. Reports of a brewing war between the Ravens and Eagles had been reaching a number of his operatives on the street.

"Luke, what's your take on these reports," McPherson asked his senior detective.

"Sir, I would have said a week ago the Eagles were out for revenge after two of their members were murdered. Now, I'm not so sure."

"What's changed your mind?"

"I've sat in on a couple of the interviews of Jimbo and Freddy from the Eagles at Silverwater Jail and it just doesn't stack up."

"I'm not following you," McPherson said as he raised his eyebrows.

Detective Adams paused a few moments.

"Boss, everything seemed to fall in our laps too easily. First, we conveniently had a tipoff that Jimbo and Freddy were the likely murderers. We raided their places and found evidence that placed them at the scene of the crime. Secondly, they were both so drunk the night they were arrested; they had no idea what they had done in the hours surrounding the slayings.

"My problem with the case is that when Freddy and Jimbo were confronted with the evidence, they were completely shocked. Not in a way that says the cops finally caught them. No. Instead, it was a case of disbelief they were being charged with murder. I don't believe they knew anything about the murders but were framed and set up."

"Luke, that's a pretty strong hunch you're playing there. Do you have anything else to back it up?"

"Boss, think it through from the Ravens' perspective. If they did the murders, they would have completely gone to the ground fearing an interstate gang war could erupt around them. Instead, they're acting as if nothing has happened."

"Luke, these bikers could be a group of pretty cool characters and want to show us and the other biker gangs, they are now boss of the wash!"

"No boss I think you are wrong. I believe the Ravens were set up by either another gang outside of the Eagles or the Eagles themselves. If it was another gang, then we would have heard rumblings of some other group muscling in on the Ravens' territory.

"If it's the Eagles, which I suspect, they will need to build up some sort of major campaign against the Ravens for killing two of their members. This can only lead to a turf war. So far, the streets are quiet. That's my point. There's nothing at this stage to implicate the Ravens. Therefore, I believe the killings were an in-house job of the Eagles to show some sort of loyalty to their leadership. We're still working on it."

"Luke, thanks for that. Who do you have sniffing out the Eagles' camp?"

"I've got Detectives Jason Lee and Simon Michaels working around the clock backtracking known Eagles' haunts. Someone has to know something about the murders themselves or why they were committed."

"Luke, Jimbo and Freddy are due back in Court in a week, see if anything can be squared away by then, will you?"

"Okay boss."

Superintendent McPherson picked up the phone and rang Commissioner Small. The Police Commissioner was under a lot of pressure from the State Government to contain the biker situation. The last thing he needed was a full-on war between biker groups in the middle of the State capital. Commissioner Small promised Superintendent McPherson additional manpower and resources if required.

Superintendent McPherson went back through the notes supplied by Lee and Michaels. The picture emerging was one of a burgeoning system of graft and corruption, standover tactics and violence to control the gaming, prostitution, and drug rackets around Sydney. McPherson felt confident with Adams leading the case.

He was the Elliott Ness of today in Australia. Adams was a thorough policeman who hated standover people and anyone who bullied more defenceless people. He was also very wary of the increasing influence biker groups were having with shop and other business owners in places like Kings Cross.

Lee and Michaels were undercover police who had long hair and scruffy features so they could more easily fit into the Sydney crime milieu. Both wore two pistols. They wore one on their waist and the other around their right ankles. They had to have their jeans and other pants tailor-made to allow for some billowing in the trouser legs so the outline of the second firearm couldn't easily be detected as the men walked or ran. They also had plastic cable ties in the rear of their pants waistlines in case they made arrests. The cable ties were lighter than handcuffs and one size virtually fitted all wrists.

Whenever Adams, Lee and Michaels teamed up they were indomitable. They were known around Police Headquarters as 'McPherson's ALMs' because of their names Adams, Lee, and Michaels – ALMs for short.

Superintendent McPherson reached for the phone and rang Lee and Michaels. He organised a late-night meeting with the pair and Detective Adams away from Police Headquarters. McPherson did not want to compromise his operatives by having them come into his Police area and be seen by people they were supposed to be investigating. The four men met in a police car compound where impounded cars from motorists caught driving dangerously and recklessly were kept.

"Gents, I need an update on what's happening with our two biker groups," Supt McPherson said. "The Commissioner is becoming quite nervous we could have a serious problem erupt and he wants to ensure we are ready for any contingencies."

Michaels looked across at the other Detectives before speaking. He was confident and articulate. Detective Michaels never minced words.

"Sir, I've been checking on a lot of shop owners and businesses where the bikers have staked their turf. A good pattern has started to emerge where the Ravens have been demanding weekly standover money. The Eagles have lately been following the Ravens and trying to push their form of standover by inflicting violence on the shopkeepers."

Lee took his cue. "Simon is right. I've been keeping a good ear out on the streets among the drug dealers and takers, the prostitutes and pimps. The Ravens have an established network of people they deal with throughout Kings Cross and the outer city limits. They protect supposed gangsters who might try and rort money from them by making them a better offer."

"Simon, what do you mean by the better offer?" Supt McPherson asked.

"Sir, if the shopkeepers don't give the Ravens money they get beaten up, as a sort of lesson. The problem is the Ravens are now starting to take on the other gangsters for turf control. My understanding is that the Eagles are now doing the same and a huge fight is looming between the two biker groups. Winner takes all."

Superintendent McPherson frowned when he heard Detective Michaels say a biker war was shaping up. "We'll have to ensure our Police groups are right up on their training and prepared at short notice to deploy into the fray. Do you need extra undercover agents to assist?"

"No. Too many people sniffing around and asking questions will surely alert both groups we are on to them. Best to play it safe and keep our numbers low but with quick report times up the chain of command if something happens."

"Agreed."

The meeting ended and Superintendent McPherson returned to his office. He rang the Commissioner's direct line and gave him an update on his meeting with the ALMs detectives.

Chapter Ten

Scott had a lot on his mind. He was finding the study for his final high school year hard, especially when other distractions came into play. The national Rover Emergency Rescue Service he helped set up wanted him to do some Media spots to help boost recruiting. The interviews would take him to each of the three State capitals on the eastern seaboard within a week. This sounded good but would mean he would have to take time out of school.

The local State Emergency Service was keen for him to be involved as a guest speaker to some of their headquarters elements to explain the ins and outs of what happened during the massive canyon rescue operation. William and Mark had been in contact with some Ranger Guides, and they were pretty keen to meet up with his Venturer Unit. Lastly, his dad had suggested he start looking for part-time work after school to help boost his savings and pay for his adventurous lifestyle.

"To hell with this," Scott said to himself. "My studies must come first, but I feel the draw of adventure." It was Thursday morning and Venturers met again within four hours after school finished for the day. This gave Scott time to swat for his history test the next day and complete part of an outstanding assignment for English before he changed into his second uniform of the day – his Venturer attire. It was hard for the Year 12 teenager to concentrate.

Scott was very keen to earn good marks at school as this was the passport for a good job within a few months. However, Scott was an adrenalin junkie and lived for adventure. Casual observers would have thought the close shave with death Scott had when he had a brush with some Russian Mafia would have slowed him down. No. Then again, he had helped rescue his best mate from a tall tree after a nasty canyoning accident, plus a Rover rescuer sent to help him. Scott never retreated from adventure. Instead, the incidents made him thirstier for pitting himself against nature. He always ensured he had trained himself for the activity he wanted to undertake. After Scott was proficient at diving he wanted to take up flying, but this was a huge expense and he couldn't justify asking his parents to help. Maybe his father sensed this by telling Scott to start looking for part-time jobs to help boost his savings and pocket money.

Scott spent an hour studying the causes of the First World War for an assignment, changed and went to school. He rode his bike to and from school and was quick to ride home. Another assignment was waiting for him to begin on his return home and after researching several books and the internet, Scott felt better armed for it.

"Done." Scott closed his books and took a breather. Now he could get changed and go to Venturers. Mike and Cameron were planning the next dive tonight and he wanted to be in on the session.

"What about tea?" Scott's mother Kelly asked.

"Mum, I haven't got time for it. I'll grab something when I get home if that's okay."

"No, it's not okay. However, seeing you've had a good study schedule this week and completed the English assignment, go and have fun and unwind."

Kelly easily got exhausted just trying to keep up with Scott. He had a good capacity to undertake several tasks simultaneously and complete them in detail. Other young men Scott's age struggled to complete one task well.

"Thanks, mum." Scott ran out the door, hopped onto his bike and rode to Venturers.

Cameron had brought a media projector from his work and was adjusting a PowerPoint slide he was showing on the hall wall.

"Are we going back to Cook Island?" William asked.

"Yes. We need to dive the eastern side where there is more spectacular coral," Cameron said as he adjusted the projector. "Don't worry, you'll find it pretty good."

Other Venturers started mingling around Cameron as he hooked up his speakers and confirmed the equipment worked.

Mike finished talking on his mobile phone and looked slightly flushed.

"Cameron, you wouldn't believe who I was just speaking to now."

"Okay, I'll bite. Who?"

"Do you remember Anne Hinchley the Ranger Guide Leader we saw on the Anzac Day march?"

"No. I can't say I do."

"Mate, she had the really well-turned-out Ranger Guides

and they marched at the rear of the old veterans. She was the one with …"

"With the big voice and large smile. Yes. I remember her now. How come you were speaking with her?"

"It looks like our little lambs have been cooking a scheme behind our backs to organise a combined activity together."

"Where and when?"

"In a fortnight when we go to Cook Island. The Rangers have a going on ceremony at the same time we are scheduling a dive, but in the same area."

"What's a going on ceremony? Is it the same as our going up ceremony when a Scout moves on to become a Venturer because of his or her age?"

"Yes. Only they call it a going-on ceremony. Rosie asked if I knew anything about the girls organising a combined activity. I said no. I felt like an idiot at first, but I quickly recovered. I agreed to show the girls our diving gear as a lead-in to a possible combined dive somewhere."

Scott and William started smiling and looked at each other. Mike saw the looks.

"Okay, you two, own up. What's going on?"

William was the first to crack.

"We were going to bring it up later at tonight's meeting," William said coyly. "Some girls who are sisters of boys at school are in the Ranger Guides. Apparently, they saw us at Clovelly when we did our night swim and are keen to meet up with us."

Mike and Cameron looked at Scott for the rest of the story, but the teenager looked away.

William continued. "The Rangers have heard about us through our exploits with the Russian mafia, our canyon trip, and Media publicity over the Rover Emergency Rescue Service. The girls are keen to have some activities with us and more importantly, for us to teach them skills for adventurous activities."

Mike was taken back. He knew his Venturer Unit was well known now within the community as this was being reflected in the number of enquiries from parents about their sons and daughters joining his Unit in recent times. Mike had never thought about combined activities with the Rangers.

"Mike, this would be a great way for our Venturers to improve their skills," Cameron said with a smile.

"How so?"

"Well, the boys would have to show they actually know what they are doing to an outside group. This will force them to brush up on several things from knotting, rope work and even basic diving knowledge. They can teach the girls and therefore what they do would be a great reinforcement of their skills and confirmation they know them."

"Cameron, I knew there was more to you than meets the eye. I hear a cunning plan being developed for skills rather than boy meets girl for fun."

"Mike, you're right on."

"Okay, lads. Let's get our meeting underway and have the whole Unit help work out the details of our own going up ceremony with one of our Scouts and the Ranger skills day."

Scott and Mike broke out in large smiles and went over to the various Venturer groups within the hall to get them ready for the opening ceremony. When the boys had moved away, Cameron leant closer to Mike for a quiet talk.

"Mike, this activity will do the whole Unit a lot of good and open up a new world for us. It might also bring Scott out of his shell a bit more."

"Yes. I've noticed since all the glaring publicity over his canyon rescues, he has taken a back seat in organising activities."

"I think he's worried people believe he is only out to promote himself ..."

"Well, they couldn't be more wrong, could they? A couple of Rover Crews have asked Scott to come and talk with them about his exploits, but he has declined saying he had too much study to do."

Mike looked across the hall and saw Scott talking with Brett and William.

"Maybe it's time we had another camp somewhere. Have a think about it, Cameron. We could even probably invite the Rangers."

Mike's face lit up and Cameron knew where his former Venturer Leader was going. He was looking for another way to help grow and develop his Venturers using the Ranger Guides as the hook.

It had been a productive Venturer meeting. Cameron had shown his slide presentation of diving around the other side of Cook Island to what the Venturers had already done; the Unit organised the next scuba dive and nutted out the going up ceremony for one of their Scouts who was turning 15 and very keen to join the bigger boys. Mike and Cameron had given the green light for the boys to organise the mixed activity with the Rangers.

The only sticking point had been from Mark and Ian who were concerned they could organise an intense skills activity and then find the Rangers and Venturers really didn't get along with each other too well. Unit Chairman Peter solved the problem. He proposed a formal dining night at the local McDonald's restaurant next week as a lead-in to the diving day. This would serve as an ice breaker and allow everyone to have a lot of fun together before they undertook their combined skills activity.

The Venturers loved the formal Maccas nights. Each of the boys and their leader would dress in tuxedos they had either borrowed from their father or families or they went out to the local second-hand clothing stores and bought a dinner suit. Next, each participant had to bring silverware, a candelabrum with candles if they had one, a small tablecloth and a cloth napkin. Mike sometimes wore his Army mess kit for variety which was a real attention grabber among the usual T-shirt and jeans customers who would stand in awe as he was served or watched as he slowly consumed his meal as if he was at a fine dining restaurant somewhere else.

Someone eating a McDonald's meal with a silver knife and fork was not an everyday event. Sometimes, a couple of the Venturers would act as waiters with white napkins draped over their arms and serve their leader his meal and patiently assist with each course – even pour his soft drink from a beautiful decanter. All was done to promote an effect within the restaurant.

William was directed to organise the formal Maccas night with the Venturers and started his telephone networking with the Ranger Guides before the meeting was over. Within thirty minutes, Rosie was telephoning Mike.

"You have to be joking, don't you? A formal night, dressed up to the nines at some local McDonald's restaurant?" Rosie said down the line to Mike.

The Venturer Leader started laughing. He was impressed with the leadership style of Rosie with her girls and the laconic way she spoke.

"Rosie, think of it as an adventurous form of dress-up we all used to play when we were little people. This time, our Units get to play like adults, look like adults but will still be kids at heart under all their make-up and finery."

"We've heard about your exploits in the wilds, and this sounds like one of them."

"No. This is the time we live a night of fantasy and fun. It allows the kids to play-act as grownups, look like grownups but have all the trappings of youth. It's a fun night and one worth taking a lot of photos for your website."

"Alright, Mike. We'll be there ... on one condition."

"Rosie, what do you need?"

"A hand setting up our website."

"Done. William and Ian are experts at this and can assist a couple of your girls to get your site up and running. You can use the formal Maccas night as the lead-in with photos of your Unit at play. This could be followed by ..."

"Photos of our going on ceremony at Cook Island and the pre-dive instruction."

"Done. I'll sort it and get back to you via e-mail." The two leaders rang off. Each was sort of comfortable with the upcoming event.

Both Units had hall nights planned for the following week but cancelled them instead of the combined formal Maccas night. Dramas played out in both camps as the girls and boys organised what to wear, what to bring and even how they would arrive.

One group was keen to arrive in a parent's Mercedes Benz via the drive-through and order their meal by intercom. They then wanted to slowly enter the restaurant and organise themselves. Others wanted to walk along the drive-through in their formal attire and order their meals – without a vehicle. Most opted for setting up their tables in the outside eating areas, lighting their candelabra and taking turns ordering their meals so someone was near the naked flames at all times.

Mike and Cameron had e-mailed the boys to bring a single, nice flower each from their gardens for the Ranger Guides. Some of the boys went out of their way to take single flower vases so the flowers could decorate the tables. Cameron needed a new dinner suit. He had outgrown the one he used to use as a Venturer with Mike. He organised for Scott to go with him to a local church second-hand clothing store. Both were in luck. They were able to buy complete dinner suits for $25 and $30 each. Cameron's was dearer as it had a white waistcoat and long tails like an orchestra conductor would wear.

"Cameron, you look more like Tchaikovsky than a Rover in that get-up," Scott said. "You only need a baton to complete your suit."

"You mean my attire, young man."

"Excuse me Excellency, I do beg pardon."

Both laughed as Cameron strutted in front of the dressing mirror and pretended to strike up the orchestra. He used his pen as a baton and waved it around slowly and rhythmically as the imaginary orchestra played out its beautiful sound. Scott had managed to buy the usual black trousers with black stripes down the sides and the black coat with the black outer lining around the outside breast pocket.

"Mate, you look a million dollars in your suit," Cameron said as he turned from the mirror and faced Scott.

The Venturer had morphed into a young man. It was a good feeling for Cameron. Here was the Venturer who had joined Mike's Unit as a playful young 15-year-old. The boy had almost grown into a man and been subjected to events that had extraordinary outcomes. Cameron smiled. He could see why Mike enjoyed these special times with his Venturers so much as he saw a whole new dimension to the teenagers he helped organise activities for in Venturers. He ruffled Scott's hair.

"I think you need some gel for those locks of yours. Do you have any at home?"

"Yeah. My brother has some he lets me use."

"Good. Talk to your mum and get her to put some gel in your hair and help you style it a bit. The girls will love it!"

The pair laughed as they made their way home with their loot. The phone companies made a motza from both the Ranger Guides and the Venturers during the week with the amount of landline and mobile phone calls between each other. The boys had agreed not to drive through McDonald's in a parents' Mercedes Benz. A group of Venturers and Ranger Guides teamed up to walk through the drive-through and order their meals when all were assembled.

Rosie and her five Ranger Guides were nothing less than resplendent in their three-quarter dresses; beautifully made-up hair and make-up. The girls were transformed into young socialites awaiting their entrance at a debutante's ball. The boys similarly morphed into their next age bracket but couldn't hide behind their slim builds, short hair and huge boyish smiles. Mike and Cameron arrived together. Cameron alighted from his car and went to the rear passenger door and opened it to retrieve his tailed coat. The conductor had arrived. Mike on the other hand chose to dress down for the night and wore his black dinner suit, red cummerbund, red bow tie and white shirt. The boys were a bit disappointed as they expected Mike to turn up in military mess uniform.

Peter went and greeted the pair. "Mike, where's your Army gear?"

"It's at home. Tonight is really a night for the Ranger Guides to shine. We'll have other times to pull it out of mothballs."

"Sir, not an issue. Cameron, that is one hell of a dinner suit. Did it belong to Johann Strauss?"

"Hardly, Mr Chairman. However, it was nice of you to notice." Cameron and Mike made their way across the car park to where Rosie and the girls were standing with their gear.

Mike had a white rose in one hand and a bag with his dinner equipment in the other. "Enchanté, Madame. I'm glad you found this exquisite restaurant so readily." He then gave Rosie the flower and kissed her right hand. The chivalrous act made Rosie blush.

"Kind sir, thank you. I shall treasure this rose always .... Well, at least until it dies." The pair started laughing. The ice was more than broken and real fun could begin. Mike escorted Rosie to the outside dining area. He then opened his bag and took out a crisply ironed maroon tablecloth, a dinner plate, napkin holder and napkin, a beautiful lead crystal goblet and silver knife, fork and spoon. He also took out a matching coffee cup and saucer and silver teaspoon; a small candelabra with two candles and a gas lighter. Rosie was impressed. Mike then lit the candles before reaching back into his bag for a single flower vase and a small container of fresh water which he emptied into the vase. Mike was thorough. He then invited Rosie to place her rose into the vase.

Cameron and the boys followed Mike with a similar display of cutlery and dinnerware. Rosie and the girls were not to be outdone. When the boys had finished setting themselves up Rosie and the girls started taking out their tablecloths, napkins, dinner and silverware.

Some even had electronic candelabra that needed only switching on with buttons. The girls also placed doilies under the vases brought by the boys to protect the tablecloths. All was ready. The crowd in the main dining area was agog at the formal attire of the Venturers and Ranger Guides and the beautifully dressed tables. When the Venturers escorted the Rangers into the dining area the crowd applauded, and the staff opened a special service lane for the high society diners. The teenagers lapped it up with grace and aplomb.

The young restaurant staff was full of smiles and got behind the play-acting too. They said they would serve the Venturers and Rangers with their meals. This made it easier for the well-dressed teenagers to take their seats. The store manager saw what was happening and spoke to Mike and Rosie. He agreed to host the Venturers and Ranger Guides and dimmed the lights in the outside dining area for better effect. The scene was set like a comic opera. The outside dining area had been turned into a swish-looking restaurant. Within minutes, the meals for the diners arrived.

Mike took the lead. He carefully unwrapped his burger and placed it on his plate, along with his fries. Next, he poured his soft drink into his fine lead crystal goblet. He picked up the wrappers and packets for him and Rosie and placed them in the litter bin and returned to his table, ready to eat. Mike looked at Cameron and nodded. Rosie saw the two acknowledge each other and started wondering if something was awry. Cameron made a discreet phone call and sat back to watch the fun and games.

It started from the car park and grew louder. The sound of violins playing started resonating throughout the outside dining area. A lone young man dressed in a dinner suit and carrying a large portable CD music player on his shoulders appeared and slowly walked over to Cameron and joined him at his table.

"What the hell is that noise?" Brett bleated out between bites.

"Ladies and gentlemen, for your fine dining entertainment. I would like to introduce Paul Hanlon from my Rover Crew who will provide our beautiful music tonight." Paul gave a little wave and sat opposite Cameron. A waitress quickly brought him his pre-ordered meal and Cameron gave him a set of dinnerware and silverware to use.

The looks on the Venturers and Ranger Guides said it all. Cameron was inserting music into the evening. However, it was from another era! The talking amongst the Venturers and Ranger Guides picked up as the music continued to play. The teenagers kept looking at Cameron and Paul and then across to Mike and Rosie. This was not their style of music and it showed on their faces. Mike and Rosie on the other hand were loving the occasion. Nothing like a quiet candlelit dinner, albeit, with all the kids along.

Paul took his cue from Cameron when the desserts were delivered and switched the music to more modern pop. The noise level from the Venturers and Ranger Guides increased dramatically. Mandy and Liane stood up and started dancing in the open area between the tables. The boys stayed rooted in their seats afraid to join the girls in case they made a fool of themselves.

Mandy reached over to Scott and grabbed his hand and pulled him up to dance at the same time as Liane grabbed William's hand. Mike and Rosie joined in, and the rest of the Venturers and Ranger Guides followed suit leaving Cameron and Paul to take photos of the event. The McDonald's staff lined the inside dining area windows to watch the dancing. The night ended too quickly with the obligatory parent pick-up at 9.30 pm.

Mike escorted Rosie to her car after the last of the Ranger

Guides had been picked up. The couple seemed to have hit it off well together.

"Thanks for organising tonight. The girls and I loved it."

"Rosie it was a pleasure to meet you again. This time in a more fun way." The smile on Mike's face was large. "Next weekend should be pretty good. You know we could combine our going up and going on ceremonies if you wanted to. It's another way to further share the day."

"Mike let me talk with the girls and I'll get back to you. I'll phone you soon."

Rosie then drove off leaving Mike, Cameron, Paul and the Venturers still in the car park. They had organised a later parent pick-up so they could discuss the night.

"Paul, you really had us going at first," Brett said with a cheesy smile. "When I heard the violins playing, I thought for sure I would see some ballroom dancers pop around the corner."

"Well, it was done for Mike. Cameron suggested we should give Rosie more of a good time than a heavy time with music ... sort of helps pave the way for future combined activities."

Scott was laughing. "There was no way you would have played violin music all night for us. It just didn't make sense. However, it did lighten the moment."

Mark and William laughed and pointed to Scott.

"Scott you and Mandy seemed to have hit it off pretty well," Mark said with a wink to William.

"Yeah, mate. For a moment, it looked pretty intense between you two."

"William, I was caught out. What else do you do when a nice girl takes your hand and wants you to dance?"

"Ahh Scott, do I detect a flicker of romance behind those green eyes of yours?"

"Well, she is nice and a good dancer to boot."

"We'll have to watch you two!"

William put one arm around Scott and ruffled his mate's hair with the other. The two smiled and laughed. The Venturers' parents started to arrive and saved Scott from any more embarrassment about Mandy. Mike and Cameron had watched and listened to the exchange with interest.

"You know Mike, I sense a change in the wind direction."

"Yes, I think some of our boys are starting to become young men. Mmm, next weekend should be quite interesting."

Paul caught up with Mike and Cameron and showed them the photos he took on his digital camera. "Guys have a look at this … it has to be the best of the night."

Paul showed the pair an image of Scott and Mandy in a ballroom dancing pose with lit candelabra in the foreground and soft security lights adding a glow to a flowering bush in the background.

"I think that's the one for our web page. I'll also send a copy over to Rosie … I'm sure the girls will like it."

Chapter Eleven

Unrest had been fomenting for some time in the Eagle's camp. It just had not added up that Eagle's members Gordon Bennett and John Roberts had turned to petty crime and driven in a car to a farmer's property to steal. It was also highly unlikely the pair had been involved in ripping off the Eagles by pocketing the money raised by their standover tactics on shop owners. Either way, they did not deserve to be executed.

Gary Herdman had been with the Eagles for more than 10 years. He wanted to leave the group and restart his life. The problem was he couldn't afford it. Bikers in other "outlawed motorcycle gangs" who tried to leave either had to buy their way out with a huge donation or were forced to stay members for decades. Those that just left and tried to live new lives were sometimes hunted down by their former gang members.

Gary didn't have the savings required to make a "donation" so he kept his mouth shut and quietly carried on. Both he and Andy Hill had been closely watching Rick Lane and their Sergeant at Arms, Benny. Both members suspected the club President and his offsider wanted to raise the club profile any way they could. They also believed the Ravens had nothing to do with the deaths of their own club members. The two bikers often had long chat sessions together and tonight was no different.

Gary had organised a fire in a 44-gallon drum in his backyard so he and Andy could share a few drinks and keep warm too.

"About time you arrived," Gary said as he opened his drink cooler and passed Andy a small bottle of beer.

"Thanks, mate. I'm looking forward to this after the ride."

"Why? What happened?"

"Oh, damn kids. I rounded a corner and a couple of teenagers were playing soccer across the road. I don't think they saw me and they kicked a ball across the road and nearly wiped me out."

"Did you say a few nice words?"

"Mate. When they realised they had nearly hit me, saw the bike and the angry look, they ran like bats out of hell. I don't think they'll be playing there again in a hurry."

The bikers laughed as they started drinking their beer and eating the bar snacks Gary had prepared. The two had been friends for around five years and had been involved in several stoushes with each other and wild brawls after long drinking sessions with other Eagle members.

"My money is on Benny as the one who set Gordon and John up in some way and then either killed them or had them killed by outside contractors," Gary said as he put some more wood into the metal drum.

"I think you are right. I'd also be sure Rick was in on it too as those two have been as thick as thieves since we started cutting in on Raven's territory."

"Yeah. When you look at it from afar, they have been keeping close company a lot these days."

"At the wake we had for Gordon and John, I watched as they went out of the clubhouse to look at Benny's bike. The pair lowered their voices quite a bit as they inspected the bike. I'm sure they had a hand in it in some way."

"Proving it will be the hardest."

Andy picked up some more wood and fed the fire. The flames jumped and the shadows in the backyard danced as the fire settled with the new load on top.

"You know Gary, the only ones who could have carried off the murders other than our own blokes would be the Henchmen."

"That cut-throat bunch of thieves!"

"Yes. If you think about it for a minute, it all adds up. If Benny and Rick got the Henchmen to kill Gordo and John, then there would be no specific traces back to the Eagles."

"Go on."

"Well, the Henchmen play a pretty cool game. What if they helped engineer the plot to have Gordo and John killed and then carried out the deed? This would mean a war between the Ravens and ourselves with several of us either being killed, injured, jailed or all three ..."

Gary was transfixed by the depth of the conversation and the glow of the fire. Without even blinking, he finished the sentence for Andy. " ... and the Henchmen would be able to take over our territories uncontested. Mate, I think you've hit the nail on the head. After all, there has only been scuttlebutt in the Eagles and on the street as to who did the killings. No one has come forward with any hard sort of evidence to say it was the Ravens."

Andy reached into the cooler bag and grabbed two more small bottles of beer. "I spoke to both Michelle and Melissa, Gordon and John's women. Both say the boys received some sort of strange phone call before they went out and never came back."

Gary was more than concerned now. He had wanted to know why the two men had not ridden their bikes the night they were killed. Also, who would have called the two men and with what story to make them drive to the farm. His mind was racing. "Andy, I think I know someone who can help us. He works for one of the phone companies and might be able to get me a number."

"What number are you after?"

"The one that rang our friends and organised for them to drive to the farm."

"Well, Benny said he believed our guys had met the Ravens and they had called them to the farm to give them something."

"Something my foot! Ravens in a million years! I don't believe the Ravens want a fight with us any more than we do with them. However, I'll believe anything at the moment until we can get some concrete proof and that includes the Henchmen being involved."

"I'll drink to that."

Gary played with the fire again and placed another small log on top sending an array of red cinders and sparks towards the sky.

"I think it might be worth putting some quiet feelers out as to what the Henchmen are up to in Adelaide. Also, to see if any of them have been missing lately."

"Missing?"

"Yeah. Over here killing our club members."

"Good move sunshine. Make the calls."

Chapter Twelve

Roger called a full meeting of the Ravens at Ken's place. He was Ken's right-hand man and lieutenant. If anything happened to Ken, Roger would take over immediately, so when he spoke, he did so with authority. Around forty bikers started arriving at Ken's property, south of Sydney. His backyard soon became a loud and busy area as more and more bikers made their way through the security gates at the front of the property and drove around to the rear where the shipping containers were located.

"Guys, grab a beer and come inside," Roger said when his watch read 6 pm. "We need to work out a few things."

The Ravens were always cautious about speaking too plainly outside the containers in case prying eyes were around. The bikers grabbed a couple of small bottles of beer each and filed into the main container. They made their way to the rear and down the stairs into the air-conditioned buried containers where more alcohol awaited them in fridges. Once the group was seated Roger took the floor.

"Thanks for coming. Events have started moving around us and we need to update everyone on what is happening and why," Roger said as looked around the room.

"Most of you would have been interviewed by the cops

concerning the killing of the two Eagles boys. If you haven't, then it's probably only a matter of time."

Roger went on to describe a hardening of resistance by shop and business owners to paying the weekly standover money the Ravens collected. Also, how the shop owners were complaining about having to pay two biker gangs for the same protection.

"Our problem is the Eagles are trying to not only fit us for the killings but also muscle in on our turf."

Damian raised his hand like a schoolboy and then quickly spoke out. "The way to stop the double payments for the shop owners is to eliminate the competition. We take on the Eagles once and for all so our patch of turf becomes our own again!"

Damian's reply started an avalanche of outpourings from the assembled bikers. Small cliques stood and started talking to each other to work out their collective response. In essence, Damian had just called for war with the Eagles. The question was, did the Ravens want a war or were they willing to solve their issues other ways. The cacophony raised to a large crescendo as various groups or cliques of the Ravens started shouting at each other. Ravens President, Ken Street calmly walked over to his sound system and turned it on. He had pre-programmed a sound effects CD and pushed play. The loud reports of multiple heavy machine gun fire echoed around the container, sending bikers to the floor and reaching inside their vests for weapons.

"Sorry guys. I knew the machine gun sounds would get your attention very quickly," Ken said as he took the centre floor.

"What Damian has just asked for, is war with the Eagles that would have the State Protection Police and other security agencies all over us like a rash. The question we have to ask ourselves is, are we ready for war at this stage? We may want to take immediate and hard action, but is an all-out war the answer or are there other things we can do to solve the problems?"

Tim took off his wig and stood up. He looked around the container and saw the expressions on his fellow bikers. "We have to talk about what action to take. However, I also want to talk about two other things. Firstly, I have scouted a newer, bigger place we could use either for a headquarters or a temporary headquarters.

"Secondly, the Ravens will be ready to take on the Eagles this weekend as I have secured a couple of small containers of rifles and a heap load of ammo."

The room went deathly quiet as it sunk in what Tim had just said. He had now raised the stakes. Slowly he checked the faces of the bikers in the room. Satisfied he more than had their attention he continued.

"Most of you know I work for National Parks, and we have custodianship of historical places. Well, Cook Island is virtually closed down and it gives us a great opportunity to use it as a base and to take on the Eagles. This way we won't have cops trampling all through here."

A series of catcalls were shouted out around the room as the bikers started to raise their voices and argue about moving or shooting the Eagles with a couple of boxes of rifles. Several heated exchanges started and it was up to Roger to restore order. He reached under his chair, pulled out a bullwhip and cracked it twice. The giant leather thonging hit the ground hard and sent out two piercing reports that echoed in the shipping container. The effect was instant quiet.

"Let Tim finish and then we can debate what he says. It's not good breaking into little cliques and yelling out across the room. We're above that garbage! Tim, back on your feet and finish your proposals."

Roger coiled the whip and put it back under his chair. He also kept it handy – even on his bike. Roger had been a farmer's son and learnt from an early age to make his own whips and how to crack them without injuring himself, or others. In the process, Roger became an expert at using the whip to good effect.

Tim took the floor again. "Roger, Roger. We are at a crossroads in our club's history, and we have little time to make some big decisions ..."

"Just get on with it. Stop the sermon, the beer's getting warm," came the cat calls from the other bikers. Tim shifted up a couple of gears in his delivery.

"Okay. I think we have outgrown this container and need another headquarters. I also think we have no choice but physically take on the Eagles as our shop owner trade is being muscled in by them. I have a few answers to help."

Heated discussion took place among the bikers for fifteen minutes about possible moves and the fact Tim had organised for arms to be brought into the argument, before club president Ken, took the floor.

"Some years ago we put up a huge tent canopy and dug our underground system for the containers we are now in," Ken said as he measured his words for effect.

"We installed all the extra mod cons and security systems to ensure we were out of the public eye but could meet here in safety. It has been effective so far. The Eagles are another matter and we do have to address what we will be doing about them encroaching on our turf."

Ken held the floor and surveyed the scene in front of him. It had taken several years to build his club up in numbers to its current membership. His bike business had boomed as a consequence. When the bikers started to diversify by leaning on shop owners for standover money, their fortunes started to change. The bikers wanted extra money in their coffers. Ken wanted a club that made its money using honest means, but circumstances changed. The Eagles had managed to raise a lot of money selling drugs and running gaming rackets. The Ravens were well behind on their ability to raise large amounts of funds. The club often called on its members to dip into their own pockets to help the club out. Slowly the Ravens started adding standover tactics and prostitution to its money spinners and the club began to dip more into the accounting black.

Tim stood up again and tried to push his points.

"If we are looking for a place to stage a fight with the Eagles then I have the solution. If we are looking at bringing the Eagles to their knees, I have the solution. However, whatever we do will attract maximum Police response and we have to be prepared for the boys in blue and have an escape route. I can help with this."

Roger took the floor again and outlined what he knew about the Eagles and the recent slayings. He told the Ravens his police contacts said the initial thought was members from this club had set up the Eagles for some kind of revenge murder.

He said Police had interviewed several Ravens, but recent questioning of members had slowed down.

"I believe the cops think a lot of people are involved and have switched their attention away from us."

"Well, maybe from the murders," Damian said as he bought into the debate. "The cops are still trying to shut down our girls from operating and are starting sweeps of our shopkeepers looking for information. We have to be pretty alert and ready to act quickly if we get a group of the shopkeepers who start railing against our protection payments."

Trevor wanted to know more about the slayings. He and some other Ravens had already been interviewed about the two Eagle murders.

"If the cops are slowing down talking to us as Roger says and there have been no arrests in the Eagles' camp, then the only other players who could be hiding in the background are the Henchmen."

Roger jumped in quickly to take up the point. "If the Henchmen are involved, we need to be careful we are not being set up to take on the Eagles and have both our camps wiped out in the process. The winners left standing would be the Henchmen who did fire a shot – well literally."

The conversation turned to intelligence-type activities and how the Ravens would find information about the Henchmen and try and solve the riddle of the murders. Once this was sorted out Tim went back on the attack about a new headquarters. He was howled down on this front but was tasked to investigate fully how to use the Cook Island area if a fight with another biker organisation was to materialise. Tim was also told to do nothing with the rifles and ammunition until the club sanctioned his move. He agreed.

Two of the Ravens were also tasked to make subtle enquiries about the Henchmen to see if there was any validity in the thought they may have been involved in the Eagles" slayings.

Tim was not happy with the way the meeting went and decided to look at ways to bring the Eagles to their knees and also show his own club members how good Cook Island would be as a new clubhouse.

After all, he had enough weapons to instantly start a good fight – and finish it.

Chapter Thirteen

Detective Luke Adams had a breakthrough. One of the phone calls made to murdered biker John Roberts' mobile phone, had been traced back to a mobile phone used by Eagles' Sergeant At Arms Benny James. The call had originated in an area not far from the Eagle's clubhouse. Once Detective Adams found this out, he called for the records of telephone companies that had mobile phone towers in the area. From there, he was able to triangulate where the call emanated. In interviews with Police, Benny said he had had no communication with John Roberts or Gordon Bennett before them being found dead on a farm. Detective Adams could now prove otherwise. He rang Superintendent McPherson to arrange a meeting to give him an update.

"Luke, this is good work, but will it stand up in Court?" Superintendent McPherson asked.

"Sir, there should be no problems with this. I know from the phone company records that Benny made a call to Roberts. Not one, but three mobile phone companies have confirmed where the call was made. Also, I know approximately where Benny stood to make the call."

Superintendent McPherson was taken aback by this last comment by Detective Adams.

"Luke, how were you able to determine where Benny was standing when he made the call to Roberts?"

"This one is getting increasingly easy for law enforcement agencies. Mobile phones can be used for triangulation. Once I confirmed Benny had made a call I contacted the phone company who told me who else had mobile phone towers in the area. Apparently, each tower records when mobile phone calls are made in their area. Each mobile phone company knows the position of their towers and can tell us the signal strength of mobile phones recorded at each of these towers. It then becomes simple maths to calculate your position within around 50 to 100 metres."

Superintendent McPherson took his mobile phone from his pocket and looked at the display. "Luke, can this technology be used if the phone is switched off?"

"No. The phone has to be switched on for the triangulation to be made."

"Is this triangulation reasonably foolproof?"

"The system has proved pretty effective so far when we have tried to track other alleged shooters in homicide investigations. The phone companies have all signed up to be part of the tracking network so individuals can be tracked virtually anywhere, anytime, as long as their phones are turned on."

Detective Adams heard the quiet on the phone and second-guessed his boss. "You're not convinced about the triangulation, are you?"

"Luke, I want to ensure this case is waterproof. Once we move on the Eagles, I don't want to find them squirming out via any loophole."

"Okay. Let me walk you through this. Mobile phones that are switched on can be tracked by measuring the distance a phone's signal has to travel to the nearest mobile phone towers based on time and signal strength. Phone companies calculate the triangulation between the phone towers and plot the position of the phone on a web map.

"This is used daily for people who request tracking of loved ones. You know, young children go to and from school or sports without parents, seniors and others who may have mental issues and need to be tracked by their families. The good thing about this technology is how it aids us in law enforcement by placing someone at a particular site at a particular time – or at least their phone."

"Okay, I hear you. Thank you for the lesson. Now, what else is happening with our two beloved biker gangs?"

"You mean three."

"Three?"

"Yep. We need to start factoring in the Henchmen as there are now rumbles on the street that they had a hand in the Eagle's killings. The Henchmen are from Adelaide but may want to spread their tentacles into Sydney."

Superintendent McPherson was a patient man. However, he was one for details. He liked to sift through the details of a crime and look for the weaknesses. This latest piece of information was also ringing alarm bells in his head.

"Luke, what sort of things are you hearing about the Henchman?"

"Sir, the latest from Michaels and Lee is that the Henchmen may have been sub-contracted to kill both Bennett and Roberts.

This is nothing but rumours and innuendo, but we are working on it."

"So where do you think Benny is in all this?"

"I think he is the one that made the call to get the Eagles" boys somewhere and it looks like the Henchmen then finished them off. Who planted evidence at Freddy and Jimbo's places is still a mystery."

"I take it you'll be having another chat with Benny pretty soon?"

"Sir, in hand. I'll be around to talk with Benny later today with a couple of uniformed boys."

"Thanks, Luke. Keep me informed. I'll let the boss know."

The two police officers rang off. Superintendent McPherson highlighted a few points that Detective Adams had brought up and then rang Commissioner Rex Small. The Commissioner listened intently to what McPherson said.

"So, Paul, the ante has been pushed up with the emergence of evidence that a third biker gang could be involved?"

"Yes sir. If the Ravens take on the Eagles, there will be a lot of fireworks involved. However, if it is proven the Henchmen did the Eagles murders, thereby setting up a war between the Raven and Eagles, it could become very ugly with other biker groups called in to assist the Ravens to sort out opposing groups."

"Paul, our response groups have started to do some extra training at the Police Academy, so they are more ready to back you if and when the time comes."

"Thanks, sir. I think we both agree, it would be better if they were not needed but our biker gangs are pretty unpredictable."

"Paul, keep in touch."

"Will do, Commissioner."

The pair rang off. McPherson then rang Detectives Michaels and Lee and arranged a meeting for the next night. He wanted to be sure he had the latest information. This meeting was timed to allow for Detective Adams to interview Benny from the Eagles and be able to report back.

Chapter Fourteen

In an abandoned warehouse west of Sydney, a group of bikers met to discuss the latest state of play. The three bikers were all members of the Henchmen Motorcycle Club which was based in the central State of South Australia. The men were on a mission from their Adelaide-based club to exploit ways of moving into the Sydney scene and becoming a dominant force. The Henchmen were keen to increase their cash flow for their club. The easiest way for them to do this was by having good control of prostitution, drugs and standover rackets in the main areas of Sydney, the vice capital of Australia. Standing in their way were the Ravens and Eagles motorcycle clubs who already had a stranglehold on the rackets.

Rather than take on the two opposing biker groups directly, the Henchmen decided to run a campaign to destabilise both opposition groups by manipulating a major incident and shifting the blame to the Eagles and Ravens. The incident was the murders of Eagles members Gordon Bennett and John Roberts.

The Henchmen had been contracted to kill the two Eagles members and try and blame it on the Ravens. The Eagles hoped this would pave the way for them to become the dominant force in Sydney concerning the rackets. The Henchmen had other ideas. They carried out the killings and then decided to hang around to see if a major fight between the Eagles and Ravens took place. Once the Police had helped clean up the mess the way would be open for the Henchmen to make their presence known in force and install their style of illegal tactics and strong-arm influence to standover shop owners, drug merchants and prostitutes.

Mitchell Gallard studied the faces of his two compatriots as they drank their beer and checked messages on their laptops. He had led the threesome across from Adelaide and was the main contact with Benny of the Eagles. The three had driven to Sydney in an old six-cylinder sedan, rather than ride across to the eastern state on their bikes, so they were more inconspicuous.

"Hugh, any word on how the cops are going with their investigations?"

"Mitch, it's been pretty quiet on the streets. I haven't seen anyone snooping around the usual haunts for a while," Hugh said as he looked away from his laptop. "I'll be going back out shortly with Keith for a walk around, so we'll update you this arvo."

"Okay. Just keep a low profile."

"No probs."

Mitchell had initially been contacted and contracted by Benny of the Eagles to do away with Gordo and Jimbo. The hits on the Eagles members were supposed to be quick and for the Henchmen to return home immediately. The Henchmen decided the opportunity for a war between the Ravens and

Eagles was too good not to exploit. Winner, take all in this culture!

The three Henchmen had kept a low profile since carrying out the murders of the two Eagles boys. They had ensured they only used mobile phones in any contact with Benny and the Eagles so no landline telephones were used where an intercity dialling code would have to be used. This way, if Benny or anyone else monitored their calls and saw the incoming phone number they wouldn't know where it was from. The three Henchmen all had short haircuts and virtually looked like city office workers in how they dressed. This was a far cry from the long-plaited hair tied behind their heads; moustaches and goatee beards that seemed to be the hallmark of Henchmen members. These members were on a mission.

If they did their jobs right, they would be richly rewarded with bonus payments from the lucrative standover tactics and drug trade they were positioning their biker group to take over. All they had to do was eliminate the competition. The first two killings were easy. In Adelaide, the Henchmen had been perfecting the use of pipe bombs strapped to the underbelly of motorcycles. The detonation was provided by remote control keys for garages. The Henchmen had got the idea from the improvised explosive devices used by extremists in Iraq and Afghanistan. Use simple everyday components that are easy to buy. Configure them with a small amount of plastic explosive and attach the remote-control devices. The small bombs could then be detonated from a distance where the trigger people could watch in safety.

The first attempts at the pipe bombs had caused a few

Henchmen members some horrific injuries with a couple of bikers losing fingers and a hand in their backyard explosions. Police initially thought a gang war had erupted between the Henchmen and other gangs in Adelaide. A special watch was placed on the biker group by Police because the weapons they were trying to develop were more in keeping with terrorist cells.

Adelaide Police had noticed four of the Henchmen could not be accounted for and circulated their photos and backgrounds to other Police forces within Australia.

Chapter Fifteen

Detective Luke Adams was not surprised when he received a fax from his Adelaide police counterparts. The fax was an intelligence brief on activities surrounding surveillance operations of the Henchmen motorcycle group. It detailed what the biker group had been doing in the past few weeks around South Australia. The brief also detailed that four of the group had disappeared and police in each State were to be on the lookout for the men as they could be trying to set up new branch offices. Photographs of the four men accompanied the brief.

Detective Adams called his undercover team of Detectives Jason Lee and Simon Michaels to a meeting at the pound where police take the cars of speeding drivers and those that drive recklessly. He gave copies of the fax and photos to Lee and Michaels.

"This is pretty interesting news from Adelaide," Adams said. "This could be part of the jigsaw we need about the Eagles" murders."

Lee looked at the photos carefully and then took a second look. "Luke, I think I have seen a couple of these dudes up at Kings Cross. They are pretty similar but without the long hair, T-shirts, and sleeveless leather vests."

"Great news."

"Luke this is only my suspicion. Nothing concrete."

Detective Michaels finished scanning the photos and looked at both police officers. "I'm sure I've seen two of these men snooping around the strip joints and having long coffees near where a couple of the prostitutes hang out."

Detective Adams' eyes lit up as he sensed he was vindicated in assuming outside contractors had carried out the murders of Gordo and Jimbo.

"Okay. How about I organise a couple of undercover photographers and sound people to watch the hotspots you have identified? We could start this afternoon when the new shift of prostitutes and drug dealers hits the streets."

Both Lee and Michaels agreed and then worked out details of where they could be positioned for best effect. The meeting concluded and the undercover police left separately. Detective Adams picked up the phone and rang Superintendent McPherson.

"Boss, I think I can prove the Henchmen were involved in the Eagles' murders," Adams said.

"Has someone confessed?"

"Err, no boss. I received some intel and photos from Adelaide today that four of the Henchmen have been missing for a while and could be setting up branch offices in other States.

"I called in Lee and Michaels, and both believed they have seen a couple of the men in the Henchmen photos but not with the usual biker trappings. They look more like business-people with shorter hair and conventional casual clothes."

"Luke, this changes a lot of things. Have you organised for our people with listening capability and photographers to scour the area with Lee and Michaels?"

"No. I was just about to but wanted to alert you first, so we are both aligned as to what was happening and why."

"Good work. Keep me informed regardless of the time of day if something happens. If the Henchmen are here and were involved in the Eagles' murder, then we are about to see some sort of war break out for sure between the Ravens and Eagles."

"How about we let the Ravens know we are looking for the Henchmen and get them involved too?"

"No. Officially if we do that, we would then be responsible for any bloodletting between the biker groups. However, if we called in a couple of the Ravens to update their story about their whereabouts when Bennett and Roberts were killed and then ask if they know the men in the photos, that could do it for us."

Detective Adams thought about the trap the Superintendent was setting. "I see your point and I'll make it happen. I'll also get the sound and photographic people onto Lee and Michaels."

The moment Detective Adams rang off Superintendent McPherson rang Commissioner Small and asked for an immediate meeting. The Commissioner knew McPherson would never ask for a short notice meeting unless it was important. Within seventy-five minutes the two men were meeting in the Commissioner's plush offices overlooking Sydney Harbour.

"Commissioner thanks for seeing me so quickly."

"Paul, you sounded pretty urgent. What's happening?"

"Sir, we think Adelaide may have the clues as to who murdered the two Eagles" members."

Commissioner Small leant forward and picked up his cup of tea from the small table between the two men.

"The intel section sent over a brief detailing what the Henchmen have been up to for the past couple of weeks. Missing from all usual haunts has been three of their members.

"The Adelaide intel also sent photos of the three missing bikers and our undercover men Detectives Lee and Michaels believe they may have seen them in Kings Cross with altered identities and more normal-looking clothes."

"Paul this is good news in one sense – especially if we can prove the Henchmen's involvement and ensure they don't leave our fair State. If we succeed here, then we could head off a major fight between the Ravens and Eagles."

"Sir, metaphorically speaking, the bloodhounds are out and we have to see what game they bring us."

"True. So true. Keep me fully informed as the Premier is particularly keen to know about these biker groups. We had such a hard time when the beach riots erupted, he doesn't want a second major crime escalation on his watch."

"No probs sir. I'll be in touch."

Superintendent McPherson knew Premier Barry Harris would have his job on the line if the police could not contain the biker groups. He also knew the Premier had been making 'backdoor' enquiries about the Eagles murders to see what progress was being made. At least now the Premier could feel more at ease knowing police had some strong leads and were following them.

McPherson had hardly been in bed for an hour when his mobile phone rang.

"G'day boss. This is Jason. I have something for you to see," Detective Jason Lee said.

"Mate, can it wait until morning?

"If we wait, we could lose an opportunity you will want to take tonight."

"Okay. See you in the pound. Ensure the other two are with you."

"No probs. See you soon."

Superintendent McPherson showered, dressed and drove to the police car compound where he had last met his ALMs detectives. "This had better be good," he thought to himself. The drive across the city took him twenty minutes and traffic was light. Then again, traffic should be light as the time was now 11.30 pm. He started work in the office in another six hours – minus whatever was going to happen now.

Superintendent McPherson drove carefully as he made his way to the police car compound. A few extra cars with lowered springs, low profile tyres and large mufflers had been added to the array of vehicles impounded by police. The smell of burnt rubber and petrol pervaded the air from where the new cars had been either racing or driving hard at speed. The gates at the side street entrance opened slowly after Superintendent McPherson showed his police badge to a camera located on a stand at the entrance. A few moments later he was met by Detective Lee who ushered him inside the compound's office.

"Boss, grab a coffee I have some short films to show you,"

Detective Lee said as he ushered the Superintendent into a tearoom.

"So what do you have for me that you couldn't discuss over the phone?"

"Sir, I've managed to retrieve several films from closed-circuit televisions around the Kings Cross precinct. These CCTVs are located near hotels and the strip tease joints."

"Do they show the Henchmen in action?"

"Sir, you're jumping the gun. The videos show at least two of the Henchmen sniffing around Kings Cross. However, there is a clincher."

"What?"

"They were seen following the Eagles as that group visited a series of shops and businesses. No doubt to collect the week's standover money. Also, we don't know where the third Henchmen is hiding."

"What were the Henchmen doing?"

"Sir, you'll see from these films the Henchmen were dressed as casual office workers with rolled-up thick newspapers. When the Eagles boys enter a shop, the Henchmen raise their papers. I bet they had small cameras in their papers and were taking photos for when they are ready to move in."

"Have you checked with each of the shops to see why the Eagles boys were visiting them?"

"We started doing a follow-up but so far have been met with a wall of stony silence. However, I am sure the shopkeepers will tell the Eagles we are on to them."

Superintendent McPherson was given a coffee by Detective Adams as he listened to Detective Lee.

"Let's roll the films. In the meantime, have we positively confirmed that who you are about to show me are the missing Henchmen?"

Detective Lee laid out the intel photos of the four Henchmen on the desk in front of his boss.

"Sir, there is no doubt that we have caught three on film. The questions instantly that spring to mind is: where are the fourth Henchmen and where are they all now?"

Superintendent McPherson sipped his coffee and watched intently as the CCTV footage was played to him. He carefully studied each of the photos and then watched and sometimes re-watched the CCTV footage to double-check the images. The films were a major breakthrough but still didn't prove any connection to the Eagles' double murders.

"Jason, have we set up a tail for the Eagles and or do we have any people around their headquarters? If so, this could lead us to the Henchmen."

"No, and yes. We had no tail on the Eagles at the time of these guys making house calls. Yes, we have set up some people around their headquarters who are providing some Intel as to who is in and out and providing footage for us."

"Excellent."

"We believe the Henchmen won't go anywhere near the main headquarters of the Eagles as they would have been contracted by the commander and his sergeant at arms."

Superintendent McPherson pondered what Detective Lee had said. Before he got too far, Detective Michaels broke in.

"Boss I've just had a call from our operations centre, and they have been able to track some of the movements of the

Henchmen away from Kings Cross. They'll be sending us a feed of the CCTV footage monitoring the main routes in and out of Kings Cross."

The three detectives and their boss waited patiently while the CCTV footage was gathered, cut and piped to a computer in the police compound.

"Luke, what happened with the interview with Benny of the Eagles?" Superintendent McPherson asked.

"I took a couple of uniformed boys around to his place and asked him some more about his whereabouts on the night of the murders but couldn't shake him. I can confirm his mobile phone was in the area where a call was made to one of the murdered men but I need to sweat him some more to place Benny with the phone before there is sufficient evidence to charge him."

"Okay. No probs."

Detective Michaels heard a beep on his computer and looked up. The video file he was after had arrived.

"Okay, guys this could be what we are after. Gather around and let's start watching."

The four men brought their chairs around Detective Michael's desk while he opened the file and adjusted the setting. The CCTV footage was arranged with four independent viewpoints all on one screen. Each viewpoint was an individual corner of the computer screen. The footage showed the normal milling around of passersby and shoppers in Kings Cross and the traffic flow.

"Boss here they are here," Detective Michaels said as he saw two Eagles arrive outside a shop.

The four police watched as the bikers parked their black and chrome two-wheel machines and took off their helmets. Both men were wearing the traditional black jeans, boots, black T-shirt and sleeveless black leather vest with their club's colours on the rear. They looked around and then made their way into the building.

"Gotcha!" Detective Michaels yelled as he pinpointed two neatly dressed men with rolled-up newspapers walking on the pavement opposite where the Eagles had parked.

The moment the bikers had alighted from their bikes the two Henchmen had walked into frame and sat down at an outside café. Detective Michaels punched a few keys on his computer keyboard and the camera zoomed in on the two Henchmen. He pressed another key and a snapshot of the men was saved in his photo file. The four police watched as the bikers entered a shop and then five minutes later re-emerged onto the street both folding a wad of money and putting it into their jackets. One of the Henchmen was seen speaking into his newspaper. The Eagles donned their helmets and then sat astride their vehicles. A few seconds later their machines roared into life and they rode off. The two Henchmen left the café and walked out of frame on one camera and into the frame on another where they entered a car. Detective Michaels zoomed in on the vehicle and took a snapshot of its registration plates. The Henchmen then drove off in a similar direction to the Eagles and out of camera view.

"Well sir, this was a good catch tonight," Detective Adams said. "Simon can organise a vehicle check on the car's registration and Jason can issue an alert to all camera cars to be on the lookout for the Henchmen's vehicle to see where it turns up."

"Team this was excellent police work tonight. Thank you for calling me in. We're also lucky the government started fitting the vehicle registration seeking cameras on the general duties cars a couple of months ago. This will make our work a lot easier in tracking down where our Adelaide visitors are hiding."

Superintendent McPherson stood up and took a few paces forward before stopping. He eyed his ALMs team with satisfaction and knew they were more than on the ball.

"I'll talk with the Commissioner at breakfast time and let him know what I've seen and what you are doing. We keep making inroads and getting a step closer to cracking the double murders ... maybe."

McPherson left the room and headed back to his car. It was well after midnight and in his head, his bed was calling him. Sleep would come easy this morning.

The ALMs team still had some tidying up to do to ensure a wide net was placed around both the Eagles and the Henchmen.

Chapter Sixteen

Rosie had sought the guidance of her Region Leader, Chegs, about the combined going on ceremony with Mike and his Venturers. Chegs was a very tolerant woman but did not think it was time for a joint going-on ceremony. After all, the Venturers and Rangers were totally different outfits. The older leader believed a ceremony to bring Guides into Rangers should be kept to the girls and ceremonies to bring Scouts to Venturers should also be kept separate. Combined activities between the Rangers and the Venturers like the formal dining-in night at Maccas were another thing altogether. Chegs was quite supportive of combined activities between the two Units on their own. The clear direction now meant Mike and the Venturers could go diving in the morning at Cook Island and hold their going up ceremony afterwards. It would just be a happenstance that both Units were in the same location around the same time.

"Liane, we'll have to meet the boys after the going-on ceremony," Mandy told her best friend through her mobile phone. "We'll have to be quick with the ceremony and then we can go to the restaurant next to the museum."

"Ahh. A good place to meet people."

"Yes. But we'll need to let the boys know around what time we'll finish the ceremony so they can catch up."

"No probs. I'll talk to William shortly and get an idea of timings."

"Talk soon."

The girls rang off. Liane's mission was clear. Set the timing for the going-on ceremony with Rosie to allow enough time to catch up with the boys at the restaurant. Also, to tell William the timings so he could organise the Venturers to do their scuba dive with enough time to pack up and be ready to either watch the girls' going on ceremony or meet with them afterwards. Liane's mobile phone ran hot as she spoke with Rosie and then William. Finally, the time was set, the place organised and transport sorted. Liane had grown quite fond of William while Mandy had the 'hots' for Scott. Liane loved William's dark brown hair, his blue eyes and his strong nature. He had a tight, but very muscular body due to his voracious appetite for sport. Mandy, on the other hand, liked the gentleness she saw in Scott. She loved his blonde hair and green eyes. Also, Mandy saw an inner strength in Scott that was not evident in the other Venturers. It was a daring-do attitude. Not one of cavalier abandonment. This young man was going places and he would take anyone with him to heights not yet defined. Mandy was keen to hitch a ride with Scott.

Rosie had picked up on the change in her girls and was quite pleased they were seeking activities with teenagers that at least shared a similar outlook on life and lived by a code of ethics as her organisation did. Although a die-hard Guide Leader, Rosie could see the benefits of combining with the Venturers because of the cross-over of skills. The girls were great with mental games whereas the boys were better at practical activities. Combined, the outfits would be indomitable.

Mandy summoned up the courage and made the call on her mobile she had been putting off for a while.

"Hey Scott, this is Mandy. Is everything on track for your, what do you call it? A going-on ceremony?"

Scott had been lying on his bed studying when his mobile phone rang. He scanned the number, but it didn't register who was ringing. Once Mandy started talking, he dropped his book and sat bolt upright. Mandy had impressed him at the formal dining-in night. She was cute, around the same height as him and was quite smart. Her eyes seemed to light up when they were together, and he also felt a small spark ignite inside himself when they were together.

"Mandy, great to hear from you. Yeah, we call it an investiture ... you know, where a Scout becomes a Venturer."

"Oh yeah. So, all on track for your Unit's investiture ceremony?" Mandy was glad Scott couldn't see her as her hands had started to sweat. Her voice also had a small tremble, and she was becoming slightly nervous.

"We're all set. We've done some revisions on our scuba diving and will be diving on a new side at Cook Island for us. Have you done any diving?"

"No. I think I'd like to try but haven't had anyone to show me."

Scott thought about this for a few seconds which seemed like an eternity to Mandy because of the gap in the conversation.

"Once this weekend is over, I'd be pretty glad to show you

the basics. Eventually, you'd have to do a dive course but at least you can try it out first."

"Okay, sounds good. We've got a small pool in our backyard if that helps?"

"Mandy that would be fantastic. Maybe we could get Liane and William there too as Will is pretty good at diving"

The two teenagers had lit a small spark in each other and found common ground to build on. After another minute the two rung off. Mandy reached for a tissue and wiped her hands and then sat back at her student desk in her bedroom with a huge smile. Scott found it hard to pick up his book and start studying again. Mandy had started a fire inside him and he didn't know what to do. He lay back on his bed and broke into a large smile.

The world was a great place and Mandy had just made it even better.

Chapter Seventeen

Tim had not been happy with the outcome of the last Raven's meeting. The group didn't seem quite happy about moving the container clubhouse to a more spacious area. He really wanted more space, somewhere easy to guard and a place that had some historical significance. Also, he had been ordered not to do anything with the cache of rifles and ammunition that would be dropped off before dawn on Saturday morning on Cook Island. He reached for his mobile phone and rang Roger.

"Mate, everything okay?"

"Yeah, mate. What's up?"

"I just had a call from a friend of mine who is dropping off the rifles on Saturday and all is in train. Ken's cousin is still okay with a boat and special pontoon that will take all our bikes if needed."

"Hell, Tim! I forgot about those rifles. What time are they being dropped off and where?"

"I've got a small boat dropping them off on a rock shelf at the bottom of the main building on Cook Island around 4 am. Can you give me a hand to get them inside?"

"Yeah, mate. It'll still be dark so we shouldn't have any problems about being seen."

"Roger, I'll ask Trevor to give us a hand too, to make it easier."

"Alright. See you outside of the bridge entrance at 4 am."

"Cheers."

The two bikers rang off. Tim then went through a similar conversation with Trevor who was also keen to help out. Trevor then let Ken, the Ravens leader, know about the weapons pick up so all bases were covered. Tim brooded over the way the Eagles had been trying to take over the Ravens' extortion territory and decided to try and catch his opposite numbers in the act and maybe teach them a lesson. Again, he reached for his mobile phone and rang Damian, his club's sergeant-at-arms.

"Hi mate. Are you up for a bit of exercise?

Damian was hesitant at first. "Yeah, mate. What did you have in mind?"

"I thought it's time we went back to Theos and started to reclaim our territory."

"I'm up for it. When do you want to go?"

"Well, we used to go Friday afternoons but I hear the Eagles have started to go around on the Thursday arvo so there wasn't as much cash on hand to give us."

"What time do you want to meet up?"

"Mate see you in the laneway near Theos at 3 pm sharp."

"Done. See you then."

Tim had been itching for a fight with the Eagles for some time and he was hoping he could catch a couple of them trying to muscle in on his territory. He was keen to teach them a lesson they wouldn't forget.

The afternoon wore on and Tim was quick to leave work, ride home and change into his wig and biker clothes. He added an extendable cosh to his jacket similar to what some prison guards use in jails to quell rowdy prisoners. After checking he had everything he needed, Tim walked out of his home, sat astride his bike and rode off to meet Damian.

Like Tim, Damian had rushed home to gather his equipment. Last time the Ravens' sergeant-at-arms visited Theo's bar and grille he needed a small iron bar to handle the locks, a marine flare for the cameras and a handgun to cover off on Theo himself. He decided to pack the same gear and then rode off to meet Tim. The two Ravens met in a laneway around a block from Theo's. They never wanted to meet out the front of the bar and grille as they wanted their appearance to be minimal and not heralded by the loud exhaust pipes on their bikes. Tim had only been in the laneway for a few minutes when Damian arrived. The two kicked their legs from around their machines and stood up. Neither took off their helmets in case any security guards inside Theo's decided on some payback of their own following Tim and Damian's last visit.

Tim and Damian made their way down the laneway. Their silhouettes in the afternoon sun gave them the look of a pair of gunslingers from the Wild West two centuries ago, striding down the narrow laneway. They wore boots, heavy jeans, long sleeve shirts and vests. Missing were their kerchiefs, gun belts full of bullets and spurs. Each of the men wore gloves and occasionally clenched their fists as they walked in unison. The pair stopped at the entrance to the main street of Kings Cross and peered around the corners of the buildings leading onto the footpath. There were no Eagles' bikes on the main street, nor police cars. The coast was clear.

Damian and Tim walked a few metres onto the main street and then headed into Theo's. Music was playing loudly and a dozen or so drinkers were sitting at tables in the dim light enjoying their drinks and bar meals. Across to the side of the room were two security guards who were dressed in black suits and black shirts with each wearing an earpiece connected to a coiled black plastic wire that went down the back of their suit coats to a control box. The moment the two bikers entered Theo's they were spotted by the guards who made contact via their radios with management. They were ordered to let the bikers in and then to bolt the door after they were inside.

The bikers approached and the guards opened the security doors and told the bikers they were expected. A cold shiver went down Tim and Damian's backs as they entered an ante-room leading to Theo's office. They looked behind them and saw two huge burly security guards, also dressed in black with the requisite earpieces and lapel radios. The guards nodded to the bikers and then opened their hands and pointed to the door leading to Theo's office. The bikers looked at each other and headed towards the door when it opened. Inside were two members of the Eagles motorcycle gang standing on either side of a beaming Theo.

"Gentlemen," Theo said through gritted teeth. "I understand you all know each other, and no introductions are necessary."

"What are they doing here, Theo?" Tim asked.

"My friends are here to protect me."

"I hope you are paying them well."

"Ah yes. After your last visit, it took me a little while to re-organise how I do business and with whom. You'll see I have a more streamlined setup now."

Damian flinched, but before he could reach into his vest for his handgun he saw both the guards were armed with handguns and were pointing them at him and Tim. Both Eagles members started to grin as they saw their counterparts trapped like rats. They had a choice of trying to exact some form of punishment on the Ravens for the loss of Gordo and John or letting Theo run the show. Theo felt the tension and unease and broke the silence.

"The services of the Ravens will no longer be required as I have some up-market friends here."

Damian couldn't resist and butted in. "You mean you are ready to be protected by a group of people who go around killing their own people?"

One of the Eagles started to move forward and Theo put his hand out to stop him. "Not here! If you have unfinished business, then complete it elsewhere. Tell Ken Street our business is over as I will only be working with one group of protectors, and it won't be the Ravens."

Tim started to smile as he saw his idea of a stoush between the two biker gangs coming to a reality. "Theo, we hear you and will alert Ken and the rest of the Ravens to what you have decided. About your two new protectors, I have an offer for them. First, know we had nothing to do with the deaths of your two members. Second, we're keen to meet you this

Saturday and bring any feud between us to an end. Once, and for all!"

Damian nodded and knew Tim had found a way to leave the room alive. The question was: In what condition?

Benny James, the Eagles' sergeant-at-arms looked at his partner Gary Herdman and nodded. He sat on Theo's desk in an act of non-aggression.

"We know you set up our brothers and led them to their deaths. Why? Only your group will know. We'll take you up on your offer and bring this to an end."

Benny reached over to Theo's desk and grabbed a pen and piece of paper. He wrote down a mobile phone number and handed the paper to Tim.

"Send me a text message of where and when the Ravens will meet us by 5 pm tonight and we'll take up the challenge. The winner takes all. Now, Theo, best you let these gents leave as they have some work to do."

Theo nodded and the two armed security guards stood on either side of the door to the office. Tim and Damian backed out and then made their way through the bar where the first pair of security guards were watching, weapons in hand. The two bikers made their way out and onto the street. They looked at each other and then across the street to the outdoor café.

Tim winked at Damian, and they started to cross the road when a man reading a newspaper and working on a laptop quickly stood up and left. The two Ravens were about to give chase when a pair of uniformed police officers walking the beat rounded the corner towards them. Tim and Damian changed their minds and walked back across the road to Theos and around the corner into the laneway where their bikes were parked.

"See you at Ken's place," Tim said to Damian as he donned his helmet and sat on his bike. Damian nodded and after putting on his helmet, straddled his bike. Both pulled the clutch lever with their left hand and pressed their electric start buttons with their right. They used their left foot to lower the gear lever into the first gear. Their bikes roared into life as they slowly released their clutch levers and they rode off at a cracking speed to Ken's place. The ride didn't take long and both bikers were quick to ride to the rear of Ken's property to the shipping container.

Damian was the first to speak as Ken joined the pair. "I was half a breath from taking Benny out when the security guards came in ..."

"Whoa, boys! Let's go inside and discuss this. I think you have some urgent issues here," Ken said as he pushed open the container door. Both bikers followed him in and down to the meeting room.

"Okay, what just happened? I haven't seen you two so angry for a long time."

Damian grabbed three beers from the fridge and handed the other two Ravens a cold drink before telling Ken the story. He reiterated Tim had no choice in challenging the Eagles as a way of leaving Theos in one piece.

"Well, this ups the ante considerably and will mean a lot of preparation," Ken said between sips. "I was hoping it wouldn't come to this but at least you two got out alive and in one piece. What do you say, Tim?"

"Ken, you know I have been looking for a bigger headquarters and had a special deal on some weapons. However, I did not help shape what happened today.

"Damian and I were going to collect some dues from Theos but maybe we expected too much after how we left his security guards last time. When I saw the two Eagles, I thought Damo and I would be shot or beaten to a pulp on the spot.

"We can handle ourselves pretty well as you know, but with two security guards aiming their hand pistols at our heads and the Eagles in front of us ready to pounce, the odds were against us. That's why I decided to buy time and offer a final ending to the sniping and issues over who killed two of their men."

"Ken there's another issue too," Damian said. "When Tim and I walked out of Theos we both saw a bloke watching us from a café across the street. We've both seen him hanging around before and always with a newspaper in his hand."

"Sounds like a cop doing some undercover work on us or the Eagles or Theos or all of us. What did he look like?"

"He had short hair like a businessman, a white long sleeve shirt with the sleeves rolled up and was wearing a tie."

Tim had been looking at the ground remembering the details of what he saw. "Yes, but he also had a tattoo on his right arm. I've seen it before somewhere but can't quite picture where …"

Ken took a sip of his beer and grabbed a pen and piece of paper from a small table. "Can you describe the tattoo?"

"Yeah. It had the obligatory skull, but it was wearing something on top and had something either side of it."

Ken went to a drawer and pulled out a poster that detailed several biker groups around Australia with their club colours and logos. He laid it flat on the table and Tim and Damian stood next to him.

"That's it. You rotten beast … look who they are. The damn Henchmen! I thought they came from Adelaide."

Ken was just as surprised. "They do. There have been rumblings among some of the other groups the Henchmen were in town. Also, they had a hand in the Eagles' killings."

"If that's the case we should organise for them to be with us on Saturday," Damian said. "I take it you want to have the fight near or around Cook Island?"

Tim nodded. "If we go to urban areas elsewhere, too many others could be injured or killed if our little party gets too rough. This is no longer a fight over who killed the Eagles but who controls our protection rackets."

"Guys we need to call a full chapter meeting for tonight to organise our strategies and weapons. I'll also let my backdoor channel know we now have a pretty strong belief it was the Henchmen who bumped off the Eagles"

"Ken, be careful," Tim said.

"I think we all need to be careful. Okay let's work out our strategy and call our boys in."

All three Ravens worked the phones to ensure each of their club members was notified of the emergency meeting that night. Tim then fired up Ken's computer and started downloading maps of Cook Island and its surrounds from the internet. He wanted to start preparing his battle maps so he could walk his club members through the layout of the ground if they decided to go ahead with the battle. Tim was in his element. He felt like an Army Infantry Officer planning an attack on an enemy position.

Tonight the Ravens would see the value of his thinking about Cook Island.

Chapter Eighteen

Benny James and Gary Herdman were more than pleased with themselves. In one afternoon they had cemented a lucrative protection deal with Theo and also set in motion the end of the Ravens. The two made their way outside to the main street and were picked by two other Eagles members on bikes. Benny and Gary rode pillion behind their mates and waved at the security guards as they rode off. Within a short time, they were inside the Eagle's compound drinking beer. Rick Lane made his way across the room amid a lot of back-slapping and cat calling by Benny and the others.

"Obviously you did pretty well at Theo's today," Rick said. "What happened?"

Benny took a final sip of his beer before answering. "We gave Theo a proposal he couldn't turn down. After agreeing to dump the Ravens in favour of us there was a bit of commotion in the bar and guess who turns up?"

Rick started grinning broadly and shook his head.

"Tim and Damian from the Ravens arrived to try and work Theo over. They never counted on us being inside."

"What about Theo's security guards? Any issues with them and the Ravens, this time?"

"No. Theo had done what we suggested and increased his

manpower and added some weapons. Our two Ravens boys were taken completely off guard. When they saw me and Gary in the office with Theo their eyes nearly popped in their heads. It was great."

Gary nodded as he drank his beer and listened to his club peer detail the challenge Tim had put to them for this Saturday. Something Tim had said didn't sit right, but he kept his own counsel for the moment. No use stirring up trouble within the club. There were greater matters to work out just now.

"So you gave them a way out without even giving them a taste of what's to come?" Eagles president Rick Lane said. "Why didn't you give them a good drubbing before you sent them out with their tails between their legs?"

Benny looked around the room and ensured he had everyone's attention. "Rick, we had the drop on them with two security guards pointing their handguns at them. Gary was about to give them the first taste of Eagles hospitality, but Theo held him back."

"What for?"

"He wanted to send a message to Ken Street and the rest of the Ravens as to who was boss of the wash. It was then that, Gary, what's his name?"

"Tim," Gary said.

"Oh yeah, Tim. It was then Tim laid out a challenge to us with a winner takes all. This is what we have been waiting for … an opportunity to wipe the Ravens from the map in one go."

Rick looked at Benny and Gary and then the rest of his club members. "Do you want this fight? Are you prepared for the bloodshed and police attention that will surely follow?"

Resoundingly, the Eagles all said 'yes' and then started a drinking and planning session of their own. They had one night left to organise their offensive against the Ravens. Within a short time, Benny's mobile phone buzzed. He pulled it out of his jeans pocket and read a text message.

"It's on! The Ravens want to take us on at a place called Cook Island at 9 am on Saturday," Benny told his fellow Eagles as his face seemed to light up with glee. "Okay, we need a war council. Who the hell knows where Cook Island is and when can we go there and set up?"

The Eagles started their planning in a series of groups. Gary found a quiet corner in the Eagles' compound and followed up on a call to his friend at the mobile phone company.

"Ben, I need to know what you found out about the calls to Gordon Bennett and John Roberts. Any luck?"

Ben was hesitant and seemed to speak through gritted teeth. "You're asking the same questions as the cops have been. They're onto it you know."

"Whoa, sunshine! What do the cops know? Who made the calls?"

Gary listened intently as Ben detailed what he had been through with Detective Luke Adams. He explained the calls had been made by Benny's mobile phone a couple of minutes apart. Raw emotion shot up Gary like a sword being pushed through his body cutting his vital organs. He was numb. Why? Why had Benny organised the killings of two of their own members? Who carried out the slayings? Gary had been great friends with both murdered men and had shared many rides and adventures. They were like brothers to him. He called

Andy over and told him what he found out. Andy was quick off the mark.

"Benny and Rick were looking for scapegoats and a way of tightening their control on the Eagles," Andy said as rage washed over him too. "I feel like taking them both out now and stopping this garbage we're planning against the Ravens."

"No. Don't do anything. Ben said the cops were right on it so maybe they'll do something pretty soon. We still need to give the Ravens a pasting over them trying to take over our drug and protection rackets. Then if the cops take Benny, it will cause a good shake-up among us anyway."

"Alright. But if I find out Benny pulled the trigger against our two boys, I'll do the same to him."

"Agreed. Come on, we better see what's going on with the battle planning."

Rick and Benny had been smoking cigarettes on the balcony of the compound and watched Gary and Andy huddling together.

"Rick, I think these two know something the rest of us don't. We better keep an eye on them."

"Yeah, or they could be our first war casualties. Mmm."

"Come on. We need to work out how we're going annihilate the Ravens once and for all."

Both Eagle's commanders went back into the main room. Other Eagles members had downloaded maps and images of Cook Island and had started transposing them onto large sheets of paper.

Rick and Benny joined them, and the planning began in earnest.

Chapter Nineteen

S cott's mobile phone rang and woke him up from a deep sleep. He reached over to his bedside table and picked up the phone to see who was calling. It was Cameron.

"Mate, are you awake?"

"Yeah, I think so. What's up? Has the dive been called off?"

"No. It's all on for today. I've been asked to give the Rovers a hand with the sailing competition this morning before we go for the dive. Can you help out?"

"Cameron, do you know what time it is? It's not even 6 o'clock."

"Yeah, but you're a light sleeper anyway. Can you come out and help set up and then we can meet up with Mike and the others at Cook Island."

"Okay. Lucky for you I packed last night and have my gear ready. I'll check with my parents."

"No probs. I'll pick you up in 30 minutes."

"See you then."

Scott was starting to become well organised and had packed and checked his dive gear the night before. He also had his lunch made and his camera charged ready to go. The youth quickly showered and dressed and then went to his parents' bedroom. He spoke to his mother who was already awake and gained permission to leave early. It was unusual for Cameron to call so early so there would have to be a lot of work ahead for the Rovers. No problems, Scott thought. He'd be joining Rovers in a few weeks anyway.

Cameron stopped outside Scott's home and gave his Venturer charge a hand to pack his gear into his car.

"Thanks for the hand, Scott. Our Crew has been asked to help set up a number of the sailboats so when the Scouts arrive it will save a lot of time."

"You must have a lot of boats or a lot of Scouts coming."

"Both. We have around 150 Scouts from across the State coming along. This means we have to rig around 80 sailboats."

"So you have a small armada taking over Botany Bay."

"Yes. But the sailors and craft are all friendly and their only intent is to have fun."

The two laughed as they went through some comedy scenarios of the Scouts trying to 'invade' some of the Botany Bay suburbs and taking over the restaurants and ice cream parlours that lined the foreshores. They arrived at the competition's organising area within twenty minutes and started to help unload various sail craft from a myriad of trailers. Unloading was easy enough, but the hard part was ahead by fitting the craft with their main sails and various ropes and then lining them up along the water's edge in various class divisions.

While Scott was hard at work fitting battens to a sailboat to stiffen the main sail, a young Scout leant down to assist him in the sand.

"Hi, I'm Michael Johns, do you want a hand?"

Scott eyed the Scout for a few moments before answering. He noticed the boy had fair hair, freckles and a large smile. It was infectious and made Scott break out in a smile too.

"Yeah, thanks. I'm Scott Morrow. Are you looking forward to having a sail today?"

"Sure am. It's my last one as a Scout."

Michael crouched down next to Scott and fed him the battens while the Venturer pushed them along the sewn slots in the sail.

"Are you THE Scott Morrow?"

"Yeah, sorry about that."

"Scott, it's great to meet you. I read all about you when you and your Venturer Unit were taken prisoner by those Russians and locked up in the lighthouse."

"Well, it's a Christmas I won't forget in a hurry."

"My Scout Troop wanted to go to the submarine you went to but our leaders wouldn't let us. They said it was too dangerous."

Scott stopped feeding a batten along the sail and looked at Michael. The boy was being genuine and was keen to talk to him. Scott always had his hackles raised when someone wanted to know details about his major adventures. However, the boy was calm and just seemed naturally curious.

"The ride out to the sub on your board is long so you need to practice a few times along a beach before you commit to paddling out. Climbing up the sub will be hard as you may need to be a bit taller to reach the deck."

"Wow. Would you talk to my Troop about it, please? We'd like to check out the sub."

"I'll get your details after we do this and see what your leader says. But didn't you say this was your last sail as a Scout?"

"Yes. I'm due to go to Venturers next month. Thank you."

Scott started to re-feed the battens along the mainsail when Michael dropped his bombshell.

"You know, my parents reckon you started a mini-revolution or something in the Rovers."

Scott leant across the edge of the boat and looked directly at Michael. "What do you mean?"

"Well, you know when you started that Rover Rescue thing."

"You mean the National Rover Emergency Rescue Service."

"Yeah. Well, my parents reckon you helped shake up the Rovers as they had never been before. They were both Rovers and were so glad when you went canyoning and were able to get out alive with your other Venturer."

Scott was taken aback. It was a set of circumstances that helped make him a national hero. He never sought the limelight for himself, only for others. Scott looked at Michael and smiled. The youth had obviously read up on him.

"Michael, let your folks know I helped start the rescue service because there was a need. Also, I'll be joining Rovers in a few weeks."

"Will do."

"Now can you finish this sail while I give the Rovers a hand with another boat?"

"On one condition."

Scott stopped and looked quizzically at the scout.

"You won't forget to talk to my Troop."

Scott smiled and nodded. He returned to Michael and took down his details on a notebook he had in his pocket.

"See you soon."

Scott joined Cameron and the pair helped unload more boats from a small convoy of cars and trailers. The work was starting to become tedious because of the number of boats and equipment to take off trailers and small trucks and setup. Scott started humming his Venturer Unit's favourite campfire song *"One man went to mow…"* His humming was soon picked up by a small chorus of Rovers around him as they lifted and carried boats and equipment *"….went to mow a meadow."* The singing continued for a while and increased in tempo. A small competition started with the various adult Rover Advisors and other leaders as they started singing the Rovers' own song of *"I've got that BP feeling, in my heart, I have that BP feeling …"*

Several auxiliary workers downed tools and started clapping their hands to the rhythm of the singers. Scouts who were helping their leaders or parents and other children all came off the beach and milled around the cars and trailers where the two competing groups were now starting to sing louder.

"Who started this?" a man asked Michael as he was clapping for Scott's group.

"Scott Morrow, the Venturer over there. The blonde."

"Ahh, so that's Scott Morrow. Is that the same boy that took on the Russian Mafia last Christmas?"

Michael broke out in a huge smile. "Yep. Not only that, he's the one who started the National Rover Emergency Rescue Service and saved two people in a canyon."

"I always wanted to know who he was. He's done a lot for the name of scouting."

"Yeah … and he's at it again."

"Well, best you join him and give him some support."

"No, he'll be alright. He'll always have the support of the Rovers – whatever he does."

The two looked at each other and smiled. The man joined the other adults and started singing the Rover song.

The moment finished with a rousing rendition of both songs as each group raced to finish their respective choruses. A loud cheer went up and everyone clapped and cheered. Several people yelled out "Good on you Scott!" and "Well done Scott" forcing the teenager to walk away quietly and find another boat. The pace for the work had picked up considerably with the singing and virtually everyone was smiling, grinning, or laughing as they lifted and carried their boats and equipment onto Brighton beach.

Cameron walked up to Scott and was all smiles. "You are simply infectious. Did you know that?"

Scott was laughing as he lifted a mainsail from a boat and started feeding it through his hands until he reached the bottom of it. "I just find singing a tune that really helps you get through the toughest of jobs. I didn't set out to start a sing-a-thon … just creating a light moment. I can't help it if others join in."

"Mate, you're the toast of the town again. I think it's time we met up with Mike and got our diving gear."

"Thanks, I'd appreciate that."

Scott finished placing the battens in the mainsail and handed them over to a parent who was putting the finishing touches on the ropes and pulleys. As the pair started walking towards their car Michael Johns joined them.

"Scott you really got everyone going back there with your singing," the young Scout said.

"Thanks, Michael, start learning the songs … you'll love them in Venturers. See you later."

"See you, Scott."

Cameron and Scott got into the car and buckled their seat belts. The Rover smiled and looked at Scott.

"Who was the scout?"

"Aw, just someone helping out."

"He certainly admired your actions. Who knows, he could be a good Venturer in the making."

"I suppose so. I've agreed to give his Scout Troop a talk on Myall Lakes and climbing up submarines. What time are we meeting Mike?"

Cameron understood Scott and realised he wanted to change the subject. "Oh, in about ten minutes."

Scott waved to Michael as he and Cameron drove off. He was chuffed a scout had known about his exploits and asked him to talk to a Scout Troop about his adventures. Scott made a mental note to get back to Michael after talking with Mike.

"Scott, I think you just completed your last linking activity between Venturers and Rovers. I'll check with Mike and if that's the case, we'll hold your own going-up ceremony as soon as I can organise the Crew."

Scott smiled. "Excellent. I just had this feeling today I had outgrown Venturers, so I think it's time to move on."

Chapter Twenty

The buzz on the streets around Kings Cross was that a final showdown between the Eagles and the Ravens was imminent. Word about a major escalation of tension and a possible settling of issues between the two motorcycle biker gangs had spread quickly among shop owners and drug pushers since Tim and Damian from the Ravens were bailed up by two Eagles members in Theo's Bar and Grill.

It didn't take long before Detective Simon Michaels picked on the information. He had been working hard identifying the vehicle the Henchmen had been driving around Kings Cross. Police analysts had been able to magnify a portion of the number plate on a car driven by a member of the Henchmen. It was now up to good police work to determine when and where the fight was to occur.

Detective Michaels was lucky. One of his informants was a drug addict who irregularly contacted him with information on the proviso he was left alone. The addict was to call Michaels 'Sam' so he would know who was contacting him. It was just before 8 am when Michaels' mobile phone rang.

"Sam. You gonna be busy today."

"Hi mate. What's going down?"

"The blue is on between them Eagles and Ravens at the old forts."

"Mate, help me out more. What forts and what time?"

"Sam that's all I know. The fight is today near the old forts. I gotta go."

Detective Michaels swallowed hard. If his informant was right, blood would be spilt today unless Police stopped it. He rang Detective Adams and told him the news.

"Simon, thanks for the update. I was planning to go sailing with my nephew, but this changes everything," Adams said as he wrote down what his offsider had told him.

"Mate, I'll crank this up and let the bosses know. I'll meet you at the Police Centre within an hour. Can you get Jason over too as I think we'll be pretty busy today."

"No probs. See you there."

Detective Adams rang his boss Superintendent McPherson and updated him.

"Luke, what forts do you think he meant?"

"Sir, I don't know. Sydney has several old forts built to ward off the Russians two centuries ago and against the Japanese last century."

"Okay. See you at the Centre at 8 am sharp so we can start pouring over maps and data."

"No probs."

Superintendent McPherson hated going to the Commissioner half-hearted, but on this occasion felt he had no choice, so he rang his boss's private mobile.

"Sir, it's Paul. We could be in for a tough day. I've just had word from my men on the streets that the Eagles and Ravens are due to stage a bloody fight today somewhere in Sydney."

The Commissioner had been awake for a few hours with problems of a politician who was about to be arrested on fraud charges. "Paul, this is not a good day. The Premier is already fuming over the fact one of his backbenchers will soon get a visit from the fraud squad. With the bike feud on top, it will certainly make his day,"

"Well at least Commissioner, if the biker fight takes place it will push any news of the politician to the margins or back pages."

"You're right. What's your plan of attack?"

"Sir, you'll need to activate the Sydney Police Centre, so it is manned continuously over the next 24 to 48 hours. Also, you'll need the State Protection boys, our helicopters and water cannon."

"Alright, Paul. I'll authorise the Deputy Commissioner to staff the Centre and call out our troops. I'll see you in the Centre just after 8 am."

"Alright, sir. See you then."

Commissioner Rex Small decided to make another cup of tea before he rang the Premier back. He needed a nice brew to settle his nerves before he rang his political master and tell him the news.

Some days were harder than others.

Chapter Twenty-One

The Eagles had been up all night preparing for their stoush with the Ravens. Each of the biker's pannier bags was emptied and filled with ammunition brought into the clubhouse by small groups of two-wheeled members. A nasty array of weaponry had been gathered and laid out in the closed headquarters on a series of wooden tables. Small bottles of gun oil and cleaning cloths were placed strategically between groups of handguns; shortened shotguns and rifles. An armourer checked each of the weapons and personally supervised the Eagles cleaning them. He also went through procedures if any of the weapons had stoppages because of miss-feeds of ammunition.

Gary Herdman and Andy Hill paired off and were cleaning their weapons when Gary's mobile phone vibrated in his pocket. The tall biker listened intently, looked at Andy and then smiled. He had received the news he had been waiting for from his contact in the phone company. He rang off with a curt "Thanks mate" and replaced his phone in his pocket. He looked at Andy and nodded his head at an angle towards the main exit to the compound.

"Mate, it's time for a smoke."

"Everything alright?"

"Yes. The second last piece of the jigsaw just fell into my lap. Come on."

The pair signalled to the other bikers they were going outside for a cigarette. Another biker checked their weapons were still on the table and gave a thumbs up. Gary and Andy walked onto the verandah and away from the doorway.

"Andy, remember I was going to ask me mate about any phone calls to Gordo or Johnno before they were murdered?"

"Yeah, mate."

"Well, that was my contact at the phone company. He had to piece together some information for the cops investigating the murders. He just told me the calls came from Benny's phone."

"Oh hell. This changes a lot of things!"

"Yes. Do we need to still have the war with the Ravens? Why did Benny have the two guys killed? He also said calls were made from Benny's phone before the murders and just after to a mobile phone registered for service in Adelaide."

"Those mongrels. The Henchmen are involved!"

"Yes. Benny has also been calling them occasionally in the last few weeks. I'll make another call to him shortly and see if he can give us the location of that Adelaide phone now."

"Yes. Then we might have to tidy things up for Gordo and Johnno."

"Yes."

The men finished their cigarettes and went back inside the main room and continued to clean their weapons. Gary noticed Benny had been watching him as he re-entered the room but paid no heed to it. Andy on the other hand started mulling over all that Gary had told him. He had been good friends with Gordon and John and was keen to know what happened to them. A story about the Ravens setting them up and then killing them just didn't wash. There had been no bad blood. No turf war at that stage. Gordon Bennett and John Roberts had trouble sometimes making ends meet for their families.

They had cooked up some scheme to try and break into the burgeoning drug trade run by the Ravens but nothing to warrant their executions. Andy hadn't seen or heard of any conspiracy by the two murdered men to not involve the Eagles in their scheme. Before the two men could show the full chapter of the Eagles their scheme, their lives were snuffed out.

Benny stood on a chair and started to shout out. "Hey guys, we have a couple of hours before our final meet with the Ravens. We know generally how we will run our plan, but it will depend on what sort of reception we find. Check your weapons once more and then we'll go over our plans as a group once more."

A rousing cheer went up as the Eagles members raised their weapons and started yelling out obscenities at the Ravens. Rick Lane followed Benny's lead and also stood on a chair.

"We have to remember guys, it was the Ravens who shot and murdered Gordon and John. In a couple of hours, we will seal the fate of the Ravens once and for all ..."

Gary looked at Benny, then Rick and noticed the sergeant-at-arms was watching him as the president spoke. An uneasy feeling came over Gary as he listened to Rick Lane rev up his troops. When he spoke about the two murdered men, Benny's gaze on him and Andy became intense. Andy shifted his left foot slowly and gave Gary a soft nudge on his right foot. It was a way of saying he saw and heard what was happening.

Lots of questions started flowing and Benny joined Rick on a chair to help answer them. Andy leaned closer to Gary and told him he had a plan. The Eagles shouted and hollered as they raised their weapons up and down in the air. Chorus after chorus of "Let's take them out" rang out. This would be one of the most vicious fights the Eagles had ever fought. They wanted to reign supreme and be the leaders in the crime rackets around Sydney.

While the back-slapping and weapon raising took place Andy slipped outside to where all the bikes were lined up. He went to his bike and pulled out two small magnetic metal containers each the size of a man's hand. Andy placed one under each of the bikes of Rick Lane and Benny James. Andy returned to the room and was back slapping other Eagles members as he grabbed his beer. Gary caught Andy's eye and his mate winked at him in a gesture of 'everything's ok'.

Gary smiled and kept up the pretence too, so no attention was drawn to either himself or Andy. Rick called for his members to start packing their weapons away on their bikes, pannier bags and on their bodies. Within 30 minutes the main room was clean of both weapons and ammunition. An overhead projector was turned on and maps of Cook Island started to be shown on the main feature wall.

Rounds of drinks were called and detailed planning got underway to bring about the demise of the Ravens.

Chapter Twenty-Two

Tim received a surprise call from a café owner in Kings Cross. The man said he had some information that would help in the forthcoming war between the two biker groups.

"What do you have for me?" Tim asked.

"I know where the Henchmen have been hiding out!"

Tim stood riveted in his spot. This information was gold. He knew the voice of the caller as the man who owned the café opposite Theo's Bar and Grill.

"You've been shadowed most times you have called in to collect your, uh, rent."

"Is that so? Who by and where can I find them?"

"Two men have taken it in turns to watch you from my café. I had someone follow them and I know where they are hiding. The men drive a 1960's white car with South Australian number plates. They are staying at an abandoned warehouse not far from here."

"Why are you telling me all this?"

"I understand today you are going into battle with your Eagles friends. I wanted to give you a little present to help you."

Tim's mind was racing at a hundred kilometres an hour. He jotted down the address details for the Henchmen and pulled his president Ken and Roger aside to tell them of the news. A discussion took place, and two other club members were dispatched to the scene in a car. They were ordered to change into something more casual so they would not attract attention. Their mission was specific. Take out the Henchmen and leave no witnesses.

The two bikers, Ted and Robert, were experts in pipe bombs and had a couple on standby stashed in the Raven's headquarters. They drove to the street where the warehouse was situated, parked a block away and walked down the roadway with a backpack each on their backs. Both Ted and Robert scanned the surrounding warehouses for any movement or outside cameras. All was quiet and no cameras. They edged their way along the building alignment from the main driveway and checked out the front of the warehouse. No movement. A white car with South Australian number plates was partially sticking out of a garage entranceway leading to a run-down factory. Robert stealthily made his way to the car, pulled out two magnetic metal boxes and placed them under the car. The pair then retreated the way they entered the driveway.

Once outside the warehouse complex site, Ted made his way around to the rear. He eyed the back of the abandoned warehouse and noticed a series of hoarding boards placed over the windows and doors. This confirmed to him the Henchmen must have been using the front door as their only way in. Ted scanned the area well and then bent down to his backpack. He had several screw cap soft drink bottles filled with petrol. Ted reached inside his bag and pulled out some cloth wicks and started putting these into the bottles. He then rang Robert's mobile phone three times. This was a signal he was ready and would start a fire. Ted then lit each of the bottles and lobbed them against the hoardings. The last he threw into a second-floor window that had no coverings. Each bottle exploded into a ball of flame and started burning the wooden coverings. The bottle that was lobbed through the glass window was the trigger that caused the most movement.

"What the hell's going on?" Mitchell said to Hugh as they were working on their laptops on the first floor.

"I think we've been bombed. Quick get the laptops and weapons."

Within a few seconds, the laptops were closed and the Henchmen were reaching for their sawn-off shotguns. Mitchell raced along the floor to an adjacent window where the Molotov cocktail had been lobbed and looked out. He couldn't see Ted but knew someone was out there watching him. Hugh and Keith picked up their weapons and raced to the front of the building. They also knew someone would be watching them from a vantage point. They scanned the area and saw no one.

The Molotov cocktail had smashed through the window onto some steel girders and shattered everywhere. Millions of burning droplets of petrol were doing their best to grow with the oxygen in the room and any flammable material in their path.

"Check downstairs and see if anyone's there," Mitchell yelled out.

Hugh and Keith went to the stairwell and gingerly made their way down. The hoardings on the rear of the building were well alight and caused a lot of smoke to enter the warehouse.

This caused their vision to be impaired as they checked the ground floor from the stairwell. Hugh retraced a few steps and yelled to Mitchell "Boss, come on." This place will start going up soon and will attract attention."

Mitchell was seething. His secret hideaway had been compromised. The real question was who was trying to kill them? Was it the Ravens or the Eagles? He quickly grabbed a bag, threw his laptop in it and raced down the stairs to join his crew. The three of them made their way through the burning waste material and choking clouds of smoke and got in their car. Mitchell sat behind the wheel while the others had their weapons trained out of the windows. The car started and with a thud was put in gear by Mitchell. He drove the car to the front entrance and as he was swinging the car around a double explosion ripped the car apart. Similar to a car bombing in the Middle East by terrorists, the Henchmen's vehicle was blown sky high and then into a million pieces of metal, glass, and rubber. All occupants were killed in a millisecond by the force of the explosion.

Robert had watched the car reverse down the driveway and pressed the two switches he had in his hand as the car was starting to swing around to face parallel to the road. He took cover behind a giant industrial metal waste bin and listened to the white car disintegrating. A double explosive force wave swept past him as a shower of flaming metal and body parts rained down. This part was over. The Henchmen in Sydney had met their end.

Ted and Robert linked up and drove calmly away from the scene. They drove around the Raven's property a few times to ensure they were not being followed. Ted made a call to Ken Street and told him 'Mission complete'. Ken was now on edge as the actions of his bikers, even though he condoned them, meant the police would now amass a huge force and go looking for the killers.

Chapter Twenty-Three

The moment the bombs had exploded under the henchmen's car, workers in adjoining factories went running to the scene. They were left astounded and sickened by what they found. The car's burning parts had been speared into the facades of several buildings. Body parts, blood and gore were entwined in the twisted metal of the car and around the fronts of the adjoining buildings. Workers had made a total of eighteen calls to the emergency services "000" number to let police, fire brigade and ambulance crews know of the carnage on their street.

A series of calls were made to the Sydney Police Centre which was now fully operational and staffed. A flying squad of detectives and forensic experts was dispatched to the scene.

Superintendent Paul McPherson was sipping his second coffee of the day when the first calls started flooding the operations room. He quickly called his ALMs detectives together in the main operations room. Each of the walls was covered by giant electronic screens that were either showing local TV broadcasts or maps. When the four detectives entered the room a giant map of the area where the explosion took place was beamed on a wall. The four watched as an officer replaced the map with an internet search engine. Within moments a satellite view of the death scene was flashed on the wall – minus any explosion or its aftermath as the photos shown were taken some months before.

"Luke, do you recognise the area at all?" Superintendent McPherson asked.

"No boss."

"I do," Detective Lee chimed in. "It's part of an old run-down factory or warehouse complex. There are places there that sell carpets, paints, some clothing and metal fabrications. I had to go there once to buy some window frames."

Superintendent McPherson was handed the first situation report or sitrep. A car containing an unknown number of occupants had been blown apart at the entrance to the factory complex. The car was a white 1960s model and had a South Australian number plate.

"Gents, game on! This sitrep confirms the car you were looking for Simon has been blown up. The question now, is by whom? Was it the Ravens or Eagles?"

"Sir, I don't think it would be by the Eagles. They were the ones who hired them in the first place."

"Yes. But there could have been a double cross. Let's not immediately blame the Ravens. We need to have a meeting with the Deputy Commissioner and the boss of the Tactical Response Group and see how they want to handle our biker friends."

"Boss, this is all well and good but I think somehow the cat has pounced."

"Jason, what do you mean?"

"The Henchmen seemed to have been blown up. I don't

think this would have happened unless the fight between the Eagles and Ravens was in play."

"Do you think they have started already?"

"I think so. I also think this was a payback murder, so I'll be very interested in what forensics come up with."

"Okay."

The four men then went into a closed meeting with the Deputy Commissioner, head of the Tactical Response Group and a couple of senior Superintendents. It was decided to move quickly against each of the biker groups by hitting the gangs simultaneously. News broadcasts were going ballistic with reports of the bombing. Police were asked to comment on which group or groups may be responsible for the attack. Initially, it was thought the bombing was carried out by extremists from overseas. However, no plausible reason could be ascertained.

Finally, Commissioner Small stepped up to the plate and said police were investigating whether the bombing was part of a major biker group feud. Premier Barry Harris also became involved by saying Police would be throwing all they had at any biker group if they were found responsible for the killings.

Even before the news reports of the bombing were aired, Ken Street had ordered his Ravens to take up their designated positions at Cook Island. The bikers were ordered to split up and make their way to the island recreational area in small groups so as not to attract too much attention.

Rick Lane and Benny James were in the middle of packing their bikes when one of the Eagles came running up to them.

"Rick, there has been a car bombing in Sydney and we may be getting the blame by the cops."

Rick and Benny were gob-smacked. They were now in a quandary as they couldn't say they knew who may have been blown up.

"Sounds like the Ravens are on the march and have started their trail of destruction while looking for us," Rick said as he looked at Benny.

"Call the troops together. We better get out of here before the bulls arrive looking for interviews."

"Okay."

The Eagle started running throughout the compound and telling everyone to get their bikes as there had been a car bombing. Gary looked at Andy.

"I think I know who just got plastered all over the driveway. What do you reckon?"

"Mate, I think Sydney now only has two biker groups in play. Soon there will only be one."

The two men looked at each other and made their way out to the bikes. Both men instinctively checked around and under their bikes for foreign objects. None found. They mounted their bikes. Rick waited until all his Chapter were together and explained the situation. He ordered his members to ride to Cook Island and take up their positions as they planned, but to go immediately. The Eagles' compound roared into life like a drag racing meeting as each of the bikes was started and revved. The main gates were opened and the Eagles were on their way to meet the Ravens.

Nearly one hundred heavily armed police in two groups made their way to each of the biker compounds to interview the club members. They arrived to find both compounds empty.

However, traces of ammunition and gun oil were evident at both compounds which made Police nervous. Each biker group was preparing for a major assault.

The question on everyone's lips was where?

Chapter Twenty-Four

S cott and Cameron were the first to arrive at Cook Island, where they started unloading their gear opposite the old fort. Mike and a few parents followed in convoy and arrived within five minutes of the pair. When he saw Cameron and Scott together Mike was pleased. His teaming up of Cameron and Scott had proved to be a successful partnership. It also augured well for Scott, for when he moved into Rovers he would have a strong support base of friendship.

"Scott, I've had a call from Rosie and she will be here in a few minutes with the girls," Mike said. "Apparently she wants the girls to see what it's like preparing to go for a dive."

Cameron started laughing. "More likely they want to enjoy the view of the bodies fantastic as we get changed!"

"Why Cameron, how cynical you are!"

All three started laughing as Brett, Mark, William and Steve started alighting from parents' cars. Mike didn't have to say much to them as he waved to the teenagers. They automatically started emptying their parents' cars of their dive equipment and putting it all together in a row on a grassy knoll overlooking Cook Island. Behind them was the lone sandstone sentry tower, the rocky chess piece, that guarded the area. The weather today was clear, and the strong winds overnight had abated to give a feeling of cool crispness in the air. Perfect conditions for a dive. The Venturers had lined up their dive tubs and began to put their air bottles together when they heard a lot of high-pitched female voices laughing and talking. An eight-seater van came into view and the boys stopped their work to see what the commotion was all about. A blue flag with the Girl Guide trefoil symbol appeared out of one of the windows and the boys gave a rousing cheer. Rosie had arrived.

"You couldn't miss them for a kilometre or so, could you?" Brett said to Steve as the pair looked up from their dive tanks and laughed.

"No. Whatever they had for breakfast I want some too!" Steve replied as the boys started laughing again.

Scott scanned the bus for Mandy and couldn't see her. A feeling of despondency started creeping over the youth as he was really looking forward to being with Mandy today. The flag was pulled back into the bus revealing Mandy as the flag bearer. Scott's heart seemed to skip a beat as he broke out into a grin and then a huge smile. Mike noticed Scott's face light up and was impressed. His Venturer was no longer the young gangly youth that had come to his home asking to join the Venturer Unit. Mike knew Scott had grown up considerably when the youth took on the Russian Mafia single-handedly and beat them. He also knew Scott had accelerated towards adulthood when he helped set up the national Rover Emergency Rescue scheme and then been involved in not one, but two dramatic rescues on a canyoning trip to the Blue Mountains. It was a good feeling. Mike's part in Scott's growing up was at an end. He only had to manage the transition to Rovers for the youth.

Rosie was the first to alight from the van and was all smiles when she saw Cameron standing with Mike.

"You missed it guys, don't even ask, but you missed it," she said as she walked over to Mike and Cameron and shook their hands in a greeting. The Ranger Guides then started pouring out of the van and were laughing and giggling as they made their way over to where Rosie was standing.

"Have a good drive or was it something you ate?" Mike said with a smile on his face.

Rosie composed herself for a moment and then said the girls had been "hyper" since she met them at her hall. They had been laughing and joking all the way to Cook Island and were on cloud nine.

"You realise their light-hearted spirits have nothing to do with seeing the boys strip down to get ready for their dives, don't you?" she said as she started grinning.

"I wouldn't have even thought that," Cameron said as he started smirking.

The girls mingled and talked with the boys for a few minutes before Mike took the lead.

"Alright boys, buddy up and start checking each other's equipment …" Mike started to say.

The girls burst out laughing which infectiously spread to the boys and they too started guffawing. Mike realised what he had said but continued with a PO face.

"Just ensure all the straps are done up correctly, the air is turned on and you each have the right gear. You've gone through this a thousand times on your dive course and the last time we were here."

Mike looked at the Ranger Guides with their smart white blouses, red and white scarves, blue skirts, white sox and black shoes. They were well turned out. One girl was different. She wore a blue blouse with a yellow scarf that had a tartan edge around it.

"Rosie, who's the other girl with the blue blouse?" Mike asked.

"That's Chantelle. It's her going on ceremony today. You know, being invested."

"She's a stunner. One day she'll have the boys racing after her."

"She does already. When she goes on to Rangers and changes into her white blouse, she'll be hard to pick from the others."

"What are you going to do while we go for a dive?"

"We're going to have a look around the cove and then head to Namara's Café next to the museum for some morning tea. The girls should be well settled for the going on ceremony then."

Mike looked puzzled for a moment. "Namara's Café? Sounds exotic doesn't it?"

"Yes. Namara was a Guide Leader and decided to open her own café here to cater for the tourist trade. She does quite well and has great patronage from the Guiding community.

"Excellent. Give Namara our regards and tell her we'll be in to see her after our dive."

"Will do."

"Okay Rosie, I better get the boys organised and in the water or we'll miss a good tide."

"Alright. We'll watch and learn and then explore the place while you feed the fishes."

"Thanks, Rosie."

Mike turned to see how the boys were going and started to laugh. Steve and William had both forgotten to bring plastic shopping bags and were having a difficult time slipping into their wetsuits. The bags are used by divers to put around their hands and feet so when they push their limbs through the rubber suits they glide and don't get caught on the rubber edges. The other boys were suited up with Will and Scott being zippered up at the back by Liane and Mandy. Once complete, the girls joined the other Rangers.

"Who says they don't look cute now?" Liane said as she gestured towards Will.

"It won't be me," Mandy said as she kept a watchful eye on Scott.

The wetsuits were form fitting and showed the Venturers as being young men with their wedged shoulders, slender hips and muscular arms and legs, all accentuated. Cameron and Mike double-checked the boys' gear and then got them to put their dive buckets in the cars. The parents left and the boys started walking toward Cook Island with their fins in hand. The girls waved and walked up to the sandstone sentinel to start their own exploration of the area before retiring for morning tea in Namara's Cafe.

Chapter Twenty-Five

Police searching the bomb site were amazed at how powerful the blast had been. It had created a crater nearly two metres deep and sent car parts shrapnel and body parts, a couple of hundred metres away from the scene.

Premier Harris became worried at the extent of the damage and was very keen to find the culprits quickly. He was also extremely concerned the perpetrators could be the bikers who were planning to launch a major assault on each other at some "fort" in Sydney. Police analysts believed the only forts that would lend themselves to a major combat scene today were Shark Island in the middle of Sydney Harbour; Middle Head and Cook Island. Shark Island was discounted as boats were needed to get to the island and back. If a biker war erupted on the island, Police could bottle in the assailants and effect their apprehension and capture. Middle Head proved more of a headache. The forts at Middle Head were situated in a national park around a kilometre from the entrance to Sydney Harbour on a headland that had an uninterrupted view of the maritime entrance to the State's capital. Middle Head had a series of sandstone forts and gun emplacement bunkers built to help ward off invasion during the last world war. It also contained a series of "Tiger cages" where prisoners could be kept. Middle Head gained a high priority for police to investigate.

Cook Island was south of Sydney not far inside the first bay found by Captain James Cook on board HMS Endeavour on his discovery of Australia in 1770. The island had been a fort and military hospital but had been abandoned for some years because of construction issues. The fort was situated on a small peninsula which looked out to Botany Bay. Police started to discount this area because the peninsula could be blocked off and the bikers would be easily contained like Shark Island. A Police helicopter was sent to investigate both sites while teams of heavily armed Police raided the compounds of the Ravens and Eagles Motorcycle Gangs.

While the police work was being carried out, members of both biker gangs were racing towards Cook Island using different routes. Tim and Trevor arrived first and rode straight to the gates of the old fort. They parked their bikes close together and placed an old tarpaulin over them. The pair made their way around the fort along the rocky water's edge.

Trevor was slightly breathless keeping up with Tim. "Mate when did you change the plans for picking up these rifles?"

"A week ago. I thought if things go pear-shaped, we won't have time to strip and clean the weapons before any fight starts. I had my friends do it for me. They should be ready to go."

"Just load, aim and shoot?"

"Yes. I hope so."

Tim had re-organised how the weapons were to be dropped off and in what condition. It cost him a lot of money, but he hoped this would be recouped when the Ravens took control of the rackets around Sydney. The Steyer rifles and ammunition would be packed into two green plastic boxes. One box would contain ten rifles and the second around 800 rounds of 5.56mm bullets. The men made their way around the base of the fort until they found an old brown and light green dappled cover spread over some rocks. Underneath were the boxes. Slowly Tim examined the larger box and then pushed open its two latches. Inside were ten Steyer rifles in two racks of five. Tim asked Trevor to keep the tarpaulin raised while he took out a Steyer, examined it, cocked it and then released its barrel and checked inside the open port where bullets would be ejected and along the barrel for bullets. None. He replaced the barrel, pushed the cocking mechanism forward and fired the trigger. A plastic thud could be heard.

"Mate they sound like water pistols," Trevor said. "Are they the real deal?"

"Trev, take a look over the tarp."

Trevor lowered the tarpaulin and saw Tim holding the assault rifle. His gaze wandered onto the open rifle box and his eyes seemed to light up when he spied the weapons all packed in rows. Beside each rifle was an empty 30-round plastic magazine. Tim replaced the rifle and closed the hatches on the box. He went to the smaller box and opened it up. A ribbon of metal foil, similar to that used in cooking in the kitchen, was spread across the inside top of the box. Tim pushed his fingers through the foil and pulled it back to one edge. Disappointment quickly raced across his face. He saw rows of copper-headed bullets on brass casings wrapped in continuous plastic pouches with five bullets per pouch. Gently

Tim pulled up a handful of the bullets. They looked like pointy metal biscuits sealed in wrappers. The Ravens would have to empty each of the bullet sachets, take handfuls of bullets and put them in their pockets before loading them into magazines. Very time-consuming. Tim had not factored this part into his arming of the Ravens. He was under the impression the bullets were loose and easy to grab. Damn.

"Mate, we'll have to hurry. The rest of our boys will be here shortly," Trevor said. "We've got to get this stuff onto our bikes and out of here and up to the museum area. Damian and the others should have our trap ready to spring in a couple of minutes."

"Yeah, okay."

Tim closed up the bullet box and put it on top of the rifle box. He and Trevor kept the tarpaulin on top of both boxes to hide the nature of the booty from prying eyes. The two Ravens struggled to carry the boxes and had to keep stopping every few metres to rest. Eventually, they had rounded the base of the fort and climbed up a rocky embankment to the front gates where their bikes were parked and hidden under cover. They took the cover off their bikes and sat the larger box across the rear of Tim's machine and strapped it on. Trevor took the ammunition box and strapped it to the rear of his bike. Both Ravens then rode back across the old wooden carriageway and up onto the main road to a grassy knoll between the sandstone lookout tower and the museum.

Geoff and Ted from the Ravens had ridden their bikes onto the carriageway leading to the fort and around to the point to ensure the boat and pontoon were waiting. The boat looked old but seaworthy. It was moored at the wharf and had a pontoon with a gangway leading to the wharf attached. Geoff and Ted then rode back to the main road and around the peninsula circuit to ensure no one was in the shops, cafés, or museum. On weekends, these places didn't open for business until 10 am so there was still time to block people coming into the site to allow a free gunfight to take place. Damian and Robert had arranged for two heavily laden trucks to be parked on the approach to the circular peninsular road leading around Cook Island.

The rest of the Ravens started arriving in dribs and drabs and rode their bikes down the bitumen road leading to the wooden carriageway and island. Anyone riding or driving on the main circular road could not see the bikes as the road they were parked on descended from the top of the cliff line to the water's edge.

Damian and Robert counted in the Ravens and then called Ken and Roger to alert them. The Raven's point men then hid their bikes in surrounding bushes and each mounted nearby semi-trailer trucks laden with two shipping containers and waited. They placed baseball caps on their heads and watched the surrounding roads.

The Eagles were located much further away from Cook Island than the Ravens and had to take circuitous routes. Highway Patrol Police forced two of the bikers off the main road when Police received calls of armed bikers in the area from motorists who saw the Eagles riding with rifle butts protruding from their pannier bags. The Highway Patrol Police had ridden behind and beside the bikes and with pistols drawn, forced the bikers to pull over. When the radio call from the Highway Patrol officers was received at the Sydney Police Centre a cheer went up.

"That's two less of the vermin," Superintendent McPherson yelled as he listened to the radio broadcast.

"Paul, this confirms the fight between the Eagles and Ravens must be Cook Island as they were too far away from Middle Head and travelling in the wrong direction," the Tactical Response Commander Superintendent John Giddings said. "We need to saddle up our men and get out straight away. It's pretty obvious these people mean to have a serious shoot-out."

"John, I agree."

Giddings picked up the phone and rang Commissioner Small to alert him. He then ordered more than 100 heavily armed police to start making their way to Cook Island. The police helicopter was diverted from flying over Sydney's north to swinging south to Botany Bay. Highway Patrol cars were called to control traffic leading in and out of La Perouse and to alert residents by loudspeakers in their cars to stay indoors. Huge black four-wheel drive vehicles with special bull bars on the front and the rear filled with police clad in body armour and helmets started leaving the Sydney Police Centre. Their vehicles had already been filled with weapons and ammunition – enough to stave off a small army.

The police water cannon vehicle used in riot control was also sent to the scene. Sydneysiders had not seen so many police vehicles in convoy for some time. Police in the traffic light control centre followed the progress of the 'blue convoy' as it made its way through the city towards the eastern suburbs. All traffic lights on the route were turned red in opposing directions to give the convoy a better chance of moving through the dense traffic more quickly. Fire Brigades and ambulance crews had been forewarned to expect a major civil problem and to respond as required. Both organisations ordered several crews forward towards La Perouse but were told to keep well away from the traffic choke points leading directly into the peninsula area. The Premier, Police Commissioner, several Ministers, and senior public servants went to a planning room in the Premier's offices to respond to any political situation that arose. This was part of the State's Emergency Management procedures for call-outs on major disasters. Usually, this would be for bushfires, floods or other natural disasters. After a major race riot on one of Sydney's southern beaches got out of control with thousands of young people causing mayhem, the Premier wanted to ensure there was no repeat of political fallout, so he had ordered his top officials and Ministers to meet with him. They had a direct line to the Sydney Police Centre and could also monitor the Police radios.

Premier Harris was worried. If this act of public disorder by the biker groups went out of control, the Government could face a complete ousting at the next election for not being able to avert placing the public in danger. He had to be seen as being in control yet allowing his Police and other tactical commanders, to make their own decisions on the ground. In another era, it would have been said the Premier had called together his 'war cabinet' to discuss and plan the Government's move during wartime. In essence, the Government was at war – with the bikers who had no fear of Police retribution and were prepared to do anything to achieve their aims. Premier Harris had his dictum: "Not on my watch." He didn't want civil disobedience and gang wars erupting into the general population where innocent civilians would be injured.

Eagles' president, Rick Lane had a special helmet that was wired for mobile telephone calls. He had a special device attached to the handlebars of his bike that lit up when a call was received. He could press a button to receive and cancel calls; had earphones built into his helmet to listen to the calls and a special microphone near his mouth to speak. Not long after two of his members were arrested by Highway Patrol Officers for being armed in a public place he received a call to notify him. He was not impressed. Today should be the final day of the Ravens' existence where the Eagles would reign supreme and take over Sydney's protection rackets; drug and prostitution businesses. He knew the Ravens would not have alerted the Police – it was the code among biker groups to solve their problems in-house – without Police. Rick was not impressed two of his best long-range shooters were out of play. He would have to reorganise his troops on the ground to cover off.

The Eagles had started to arrive at the approach points to the La Perouse peninsula and pulled off the main roads and into side streets to await their Commander and Sergeant-at-arms. Sydneysiders were on heightened alert following the bombing of the Henchmen and the resultant Media fallout. When groups of bikers started gathering on side streets, several calls went out to Police to alert them. The map of Cook Island was projected onto one of the walls of the Sydney Police Centre and its approaches had a series of red dots on it to indicate sightings of bikers. The dots grew in number when the Police helicopter did its first pass over the Cook Island fort and public grounds. Scores of motorcycles were seen lined up off the main ring road on the approaches to the fort and behind several of the shops.

Ken Street saw the Police helicopter and knew the forthcoming firefight and its location had already been signalled to the Police. He believed his job was to take out as many of the Eagles as he could and make an escape run with as few of his biker members either being wounded or arrested. Tim and Damian had taken the group over the plans for the armed assault against the Eagles several times. They never physically rehearsed them like soldiers would, but had covered off several exigencies that could occur and possible ways around them in talks to the bikers. Rick Lane and Benny had done the same for the Eagles.

The first security TV images shot from the helicopter to the Sydney Police Centre were scary. It showed rows of motorcycles lined up on the escarpment road leading to the fort and other bikes behind shops. It also showed groups of people with biker helmets on in small clusters around the public space.

"Ken, we'll have to do something about the chopper or it will dog us all day," Damian said as he motioned skywards. "They would have been filming us already and broadcasting the images back to Police Headquarters."

"Damo, they must have known we were coming here today. We have only a few choices. Take out the chopper, hide our weapons and disperse or wait it out and play against two forces – the cops and the Eagles."

"Boss, I say, we can still do what we want if we hold the line. Take out the chopper so it can't see us. Force the cops to come by road. Any assault on us by water would be seen too easily. We take out the Eagles and get out of here."

Ken looked at his trusty lieutenants and the shortened shotgun in his hands. "Don't aim to kill the cops. Let them know we don't like them on top of us."

"Right boss. Leave it to me."

Damian caught up with Tim and Trevor and explained the situation. He grabbed an assault rifle and then filled a magazine with bullets. Within a few moments, Damian had the magazine connected to the rifle and cocked the weapon. He aimed the tail rotor of the helicopter and fired three shots.

Three police were aboard the helicopter, the pilot, co-pilot and a camera operator. They had an excellent view of the grounds and were feeding live images via a secure bandwidth directly to the Sydney Police Centre. The first shot rang out and went wide of the aircraft. The second and third shots found their mark and hit the helicopter in the tail section. A couple of small sparks could be seen emanating from the helicopter before smoke started billowing out of the tail section.

"What the …?" Sergeant Stuart Somers said as he felt the two thuds strike his aircraft. "They're firing at us … Peter help with the rudders we're losing altitude."

Senior Constable Peter Sullivan was the co-pilot and navigator. His mission was to ensure the pilot knew where he was at any time and to calculate distances to and from compass points. He had a mind for numbers and was very quick at calculating tables like how much fuel the aircraft had on board if it had flown for so long and how much was needed to complete a mission.

"Stuart, I'm having trouble trying to keep her nose even, we'll have to get out of here or we'll be ditching in Botany Bay."

"Ok, mate. Sydney Centre, do you copy?"

"Police air wing one, this is Sydney Centre. Copy. Are any of you injured?"

"Sydney Centre, no. We have lost a lot of rudder movement and our ability to hover is gone. Smoke is billowing out around the rear rotor. We have to come in."

"Hell Stuart. Return to base pronto. We'll have emergency services on full standby."

Sergeant Somers moved his collector forward and flew the helicopter away from Cook Island. Sydney Airport was not far away and the crippled aircraft started making a bee-line towards its own helipad.

A cheer went up from the Ravens as they saw the Police helicopter hit with rounds from Damian. They raised their weapons up and down in their hands in a scene of jubilation when they saw their overhead eye in the sky saunter off.

Ken Street drew a deep breath and signalled to his bikers. "We have just declared war on the Police so don't expect any mercy from them today."

"They shouldn't have been snooping on us in the first place," Trevor said.

"Well, the first part of the trap has been sprung," Roger said. "The rest of our plan better come off or we'll be carted out of here in vans reserved for the morgue."

Tim looked at him carefully and saw the strain showing on the club's second in command. "Roger this can still work if we keep our nerve. We better get into positions as we'll be expecting company pretty soon."

"The Eagles?"

"Both. The Eagles and the cops."

"Okay. Ensure our front door is open and welcoming for our little Eagle friends and then close the door tight. No mucking around."

"Okay."

Tim rang Robert to confirm all was ready and to see if there were any sightings of the Eagles.

"Tim, I've been in the cabin for a while and seen a number of our friends ride to the side streets," Robert said. "They're massing. It won't be long now."

"Alright, mate. You know how to recognise Rick Lane and Benny. Once they're in, close the gate."

"No probs."

It didn't take long. Within ten minutes around forty members of the Eagles Motorcycle Club had gathered and had a pep talk by Benny a kilometre up the road from where the peninsula ring road began.

"This is our last chance to take out the Ravens once and for all," Benny said to his members. "These are the same cowards that lured two of our boys to their deaths and murdered them."

Gary and Andy looked at each other. It was time to ask the question. Andy seized the moment and yelled out.

"Benny, did the Henchmen have anything to do with the murders?" he asked.

Benny was shell-shocked. He had not been expecting such a direct question at a time of rallying his troops for a major firefight. Rick Lane looked at Benny and then the group. He nodded to Benny who now was given the lead to answer.

"What? The Henchmen? They're in Adelaide. The only ones involved in Gordon and John's deaths were the Ravens. It was Ken Street and his boys who lured our blokes to the farm and then killed them."

"Did their deaths have anything to do with Gordo and John trying to set up a money scheme of their own?"

"Andy you are way out of line. It was the Ravens who killed them. The Ravens want to take over Sydney's protection rackets and leave us with nothing. When we hit Cook Island shortly, remember your brothers in arms and do what is expected."

"You can count on me to avenge their deaths," Andy said as he donned his helmet.

Benny looked at Rick and then at his troops. The time had come to blood his members in a battle that would be long remembered.

"Remember once you get the signal, pull out, disperse, and go underground until you are called. Alright boys, let's go Raven hunting!"

The throaty sounds of forty powerful motorcycles roaring into life were deafening. Residents near where the group had gathered had called their children inside, locked their doors and watched from behind curtains slightly open. A number of them had become so concerned they had rung Police. The calls were logged and passed on to the Sydney Police Centre.

Andy had looked at Gary when Benny denied the involvement of the Henchmen. Gary saw his mate seething and knew a new order for the club was about to dawn. Andy would play a part in it with his little gifts for Benny and Rick. The question was at what time would the switch be thrown.

Superintendent John Giddings had received permission from the Deputy Commissioner to throw all his weight at Cook Island. Teams of Police from across Sydney were being drafted into the Police Centre for briefings and outfitted with flak jackets, helmets, and high-powered rifles. All available parking around the Police Centre was taken up with Police Cars, Police vans and trucks. A mobile communications centre in the form of a large bus fitted out with the latest satellite communications was dispatched to a suburb at the approach to Cook Island. The Police were now on the move and a large blue footprint started heading towards Cook Island. The Police helicopter, hit in the tail rotor by bullets, landed safely at Sydney Airport with a huge collection of emergency vehicles on standby to quell any fire from the badly smoking aircraft. Once the helicopter had landed and the engines shut off, the three crew ran to a waiting police car while fire brigade officers poured foam over the aircraft in a bid to stop the fire in the rotor wing from spreading.

Chapter Twenty-Six

Cameron had led the boys' dive with Mike acting as rear guard. The group had spent time on top of the water crossing between the mainland and the island to conserve air in their tanks. They had taken a different route to last time, and when they reached a point adjacent to the southeast corner of the fort they re-grouped. Cameron put his right hand on his head with his fingers extended and looked at each Venturer and Mike. They all responded the same. All were okay and safe. Cameron then made a fist with his right hand and extended his thumb. He rotated his hand so his thumb was pointing down and the group responded the same. It was time to dive. The divers switched from breathing from their snorkels to breathing from their air tanks. They lifted their vest's flexible purge valve and squeezed the air from their vests. Slowly all the divers began going under the water and heading towards the sandy bottom. They had been drilled that once the group had descended they were to form a circle on the ocean floor to check all was right with everyone before continuing the dive.

Cameron knelt and pointed to each of the divers to do the same. Mike hovered slightly above the group to ensure all was right from his vantage point. This was Cameron's turn at leading today. Mike was proud of him. It seemed like only a few weeks ago Cameron had joined his Venturer Unit and participated in his first dive – never mind it had been three years. Cameron opened his right hand and joined his index finger and thumb together. He signalled each of the groups if they were okay. Each returned the okay signal before Cameron drew a large imaginary circle above his head like a cowboy lassoing a steer and used his open hand to signal to go forward and dive. Each of the Venturers paired off and followed Cameron.

A beautiful coloured garden of coral and sea grass came into view as the group followed the shape of the giant rock the fort was built on. Colourful fish of all shapes and sizes darted around the small rock crevices as the boys explored the serene seascape surroundings. Scott and Mark were teamed up as buddies and swam close together. Several times Scott stopped, retrieved his knife and banged its metal handle on rocks. Nothing happened. He saw some sea urchin and made a bee-line for it. Mark wasn't sure what Scott was trying to do initially. Slowly it dawned on Mark that Scott was trying to call Old Blue and then feed him. Mark retrieved his knife and also started opening a sea urchin. A myriad of fish started swimming near the boys as they knelt in the sand and waited.

Old Blue had heard the boys diving and now smelt one of his favourite dishes being served. The strong underwater scent of the yellow-fleshed sea urchin was a groper's delight. Old Blue made a large dash towards the Venturers and ignored all of them except two. He swam in front of Scott and hovered at face level. The teenager was ecstatic. His ruse had worked, and the beautiful blue fish friend of divers had heard his call. Scott opened his hand with the sea urchin, but Old Blue just hovered watching him. Mark worked it out and tapped Scott on the shoulder. When his mate turned around, Mark sheathed his knife and waved to Scott to do the same. Scott nodded and replaced his knife in its scabbard on his leg. Old Blue then slowly went to Scott and ate the sea urchin out of his hand. Mark offered the groper some more and the giant fish moved to him and did the same. Before Scott could pull out his knife William and Ian arrived and offered Old Blue some sea urchin they had retrieved. Slowly the Venturers formed a circle on the rocky sandy ocean floor and took turns to open sea urchins and feed Old Blue and some other fish.

Cameron checked his watch and air. It was time to slowly head back and do some decompression stops on the way. The Rover signalled to the Venturers and Mike to finish up and head back. It had been a good dive. There was always so much to see at Cook Island. The coral gardens were so beautiful and the fish so colourful. The dive would go down as one of the best for the boys.

Rosie had taken the girls down to the water's edge on the mainland to watch the boys swim across the channel and around to the southeastern corner of the fort where they gathered and then descended out of view.

"We should do some diving too," Liane said as she watched the boys slip from view. "This would be a challenge I'm sure we'd all like."

Rosie laughed quite haughtily. "You won't get me down there in a hurry."

"Maybe not, but that shouldn't stop us from learning and having the same fun as the Venturers."

Rosie looked at her group of Ranger Guides and Guide. "You're right. This will be a good activity to mix with the boys and learn. There is so much to see under the ocean."

"So why don't you want to do it?" Mandy asked.

"I guess I never had much of a chance as I was growing up. We always did other things. You know, more land-based activities. Guides were always more insular."

"Yes, but today they are quite adventurous and really, there is almost nothing the Venturers can do that we can't do as well."

Rosie heard the passion in Mandy's voice. "Agree. This is why I am glad you made contact with the Venturers, so you can do some activities I can't teach you."

A wry smile came over Liane. She looked around the rest of the girls and then at Rosie. "Are you sure, this has nothing to do with Mike and the fact you two get on so famously?"

Rosie blushed. She looked at the ground and then back to Liane. "Well he is rather cute, I suppose. Well, you know, for a Venturer Leader!"

The girls all started laughing. They had walked down the winding path from the top of the grassy area joined by the peninsula ring road. Rosie had stopped short of crossing the wooden carriageway bridge and opted instead to follow the rocky foreshore around the bluff while she and the girls watched the boys as they swam out across the channel and dived. From the ring road, the girls were invisible. They had heard the Ravens' motorcycles as the bikers made their way down the winding road leading to the wooden bridge. The girls thought nothing of it except the bikes were loud. Rosie intended to follow the rocky shelf at the foot of the bluff around to a small beach, up the grassy hill and into Namara's Café for morning tea before they held their going-on ceremony.

All was still going to plan.

Chapter Twenty-Seven

The ALMs detectives had followed the Police Mobile Communications bus towards Cook Island. All three Detectives had been in touch with their contacts on the street. They had definitely confirmed the people blown up in the earlier car bombing had been members of the Henchmen Motorcycle Gang through identification of the car's number plates and car chassis and engine numbers. Police had found enough body parts to ascertain three men had lost their lives. No details of the men's identities were released to the Media. A hold was placed on any identifying information being released to allow the South Australian Police time to ready themselves in case there were any recriminations carried out by other gang members in Adelaide. Police were sent to the South Australia and New South Wales border region from both States in case groups of bikers decided to cross over in search of violent action. Remains of the blown-up car were carefully photographed and then placed onto the rear of a tabletop truck. Police had erected a large marquee over the bomb site and sealed off all streets leading to the site for almost a kilometre. The marquee was to shield the site from prying Media eyes as news crews in helicopters raced to the scene to get a bird's eye view of the carnage. A marquee had also been placed over the rear of the factory complex where the firebombing took place.

Commissioner Small and Premier Harris were both tight-lipped about any connection that had been made between the Henchmen and the impending shootout between the Ravens and Eagles. A news blackout was placed on the operation which had been codenamed, Operation Marla. All Police operations were given code names generated by the computer so no personal or identifying tags could be given that might reveal anything about the operation.

"Luke, what intrigues me is who tried to firebomb the Henchmen," Detective Michaels said.

"Simon, we don't know for sure who it was yet. My money is someone in the Ravens had found out what was going on and planned a highly visible execution."

Detective Lee agreed. "I think you're right. The bombing was the biggest we've seen in Sydney since the Hilton Hotel bombing in the 1970s when a couple of garbage men lost their lives. This was definitely a planned attack that was full of outrage."

"Jason, my point is these men were among the best of the Henchmen. They would not have been easily frightened and possibly could have extinguished the fires in the warehouse and taken on the perpetrators."

Detective Adams looked perplexed. He listened to the arguments, weighed them up and then reached a conclusion. "What if it wasn't the Ravens," he said.

"Surely not the Eagles," Detective Lee said.

"Yes. What if someone in the Eagles has realised a double cross and decided to take matters into their own hands? It fits. We won't know until we get our hands on some of the bikies. So keep an open mind."

Superintendent McPherson used his mobile phone to contact his ALMs detectives. "Boys it's getting pretty close to showdown. We've got reports of one group of bikies massing around Cook Island and a swag of others saying small groups of bikies are starting to meet on the approach to Cook Island."

"How long before the main body on our side arrives?" Detective Lee asked.

"We've got heaps of Police on their way, and they are around ten minutes behind the second group of bikies."

"What about civilians in the area? It's the weekend. Surely there must be a reasonable crowd there having picnics or just milling around near the water."

Superintendent McPherson noted the twinge of worry in his younger officer. "Before our chopper was shot at it had done a wide sweep of Botany Bay. It reported hundreds of sailing boats at the Brighton end of the bay and only a handful of people in the Cook Island area."

Detective Adams shook his head. "I forgot about the Regatta today."

"What Regatta, Luke?

"There's a huge sailing competition being staged by Rover Scouts for Scouts with competitors from all over the State participating."

"How do you know that?"

"Do you remember Allan Morrow from the Highway

Patrol? His kid Scott is a Venturer and was going to help the Rovers there today."

Detective Lee quickly put the pieces of information together. "Scott Morrow. That's the kid who helped save his Venturer Unit from the Russian Mafia in that huge drug bust last Christmas. He also helped …"

"Set up the National Rover Rescue Emergency Service and saved two other kids on a canyoning trip earlier this year," Detective Michaels finished. "He's a walking celebrity in Scouts but as humble as you'd ever see. He's been given a swag of awards for courage and has friends in The Lodge."

Superintendent McPherson was becoming worried. Any civilians in harm's way were a problem. If hundreds of children were in the way of a bikie war, the result could be catastrophic. If a decorated teenager who had connections to the highest political office in the land was injured in a bikie turf war the fallout would also be horrendous for the Police.

"How far away is the regatta from Cook Island? Can the bikies get there from the island if they escape?" he asked.

Detective Adams was driving and motioned for the other two detectives to go to the map of Botany Bay and study it again. He told his boss and the rest of the team where the regatta was being staged. Together they checked roads leading away from the Cook Island peninsular road to ensure none led towards the regatta.

"Luke, give Allan Morrow a ring and see where his son is. Simon, Jason, check to see who is in charge of the Regatta and establish communications. If we need to have the Regatta shut down and abandoned, we'll need to do it very quickly."

All three Detectives hit their mobile phones and started making their calls. The picture Detective Adams had just painted played havoc in the mind of Paul McPherson. If the bikies decided to do away with each other, that was one thing. Involving hundreds of children would be unforgivable. The three Detectives pulled over to the side of the road and contacted their boss when they had sufficient information.

"Sir, Jason and I have found the organisers of the Regatta and they are on standby to abandon the event if required," Detective Michaels said.

"Boss, I spoke with Superintendent Morrow and I think I put the wind up him," Detective Adams said.

"Why Luke, what's the problem?"

"It seems Scott Morrow and his Venturers are scuba diving around the base of Cook Island."

"Oh hell! Just what we need."

"Boss, there's more."

"What?"

"Apparently a group of Ranger Guides, you know, teenage Girl Guides, are supposed to meet up with Scott Morrow and his Venturers and should be somewhere around the island now."

"Those kids could be used as shields, bait or anything. Luke, you better ring Allan back and get what phone details you can for those at Cook Island."

"No probs."

Superintendent McPherson's day was getting worse. The Media would have a field day if the Venturers and Ranger Guides were injured in a bikie shootout. If the carnage spreads anywhere near the Regatta it would be a catastrophe. He picked up the phone and alerted Commissioner Small. The Commissioner wanted McPherson to alert the Tactical Response Commander while he made a call to Premier Harris. The secondary issue was if the Police ordered the Regatta to be abandoned, the story could be leaked to the Media by any one of a few hundred spectators whose children were involved in the sailing competition. This had to be handled delicately and measures put in place to stop any spill over of activity between the feuding bikers.

"Paul, this issue is easy. I'll direct Allan Morrow to form a Police Operation blockade of all routes leading anywhere from Cook Island to Brighton," Superintendent John Giddings said. "This will also give Allan something to do to take his mind off his boy and leave the worrying to us."

"Done."

A Police Operation blockade usually meant Highway or local Police cars blocking off routes along main roads and forcing traffic around certain areas. This allowed Police to investigate areas where crooks may be hiding or going after a crime. It meant escape routes were being blocked and only certain traffic lanes were open – those that could be more easily supervised by Highway Patrol and other Police.

Superintendent Allan Morrow had gone to work as normal this day. He had had an operations brief with his Inspectors about any overnight issues, hot spots or places to conduct breath testing and or speed traps. He had been told by his wife Kelly that Scott had gone early so he could give Cameron a hand at the Regatta before going diving with Mike Hunter and the Venturers at Cook Island. Nothing was untoward. Allan was more than proud of his son with his notion of community service and keenness to help others. Scott had proved this with the rescue of his Venturer Unit from an old convict jail after being taken prisoner by the Russian mafia last Christmas. The boy then displayed a sense of maturity his father had not seen in him when he helped establish a national Rover Emergency Rescue Service for people doing adventurous activities in the wild. The icing on the cake had been when he had to take Scott to Government House in Sydney for a bravery award. After Scott helped rescue two people in a canyon tragedy, he was summoned to Yarralumla, the Governor-General's residence in Canberra, the nation's capital, where Scott was made Australian Youth of the Year.

Allan Morrow was busy organising some operational work when his phone rang. John Giddings and Allan Morrow had joined the Police Force the same year and gone to the Academy together. Allan was into fast cars and chose the Highway Patrol. John was into weaponry and chose the Tactical Response Group. They were close friends and always looked after each other. Today was no different.

"Allan, it's John, all going well?"

"Yeah mate, except for the upcoming operations for the next long weekend. What's up?"

"Allan I'm at the Police Centre which has become fully operational after the car bombing this morning."

"Do you need some extra road closures?"

"Allan, stop. Listen to me and let me finish."

When Superintendent Giddings had explained the situation

with the biker groups and brought up Cook Island, his heart began to sink. Giddings explained what he knew of the whereabouts of the various bikie groups and then told him of the Regatta. Morrow's mind was racing as he knew Scott was diving at Cook Island.

"John, I want to come out to Cook Island in case you need a hand.

"No mate, we've got this one. We'll look after him. We want you to help direct the other operations I told you about. I promise I'll keep you up to date with what's going on."

"John, I could easily give the operational work to Inspector Jimmy Dwyer so I could be free to help you out."

"No mate. This is final. You must look after the operational side of your area while I look after mine. I've never let you down in the past and I won't now."

"Okay. Thanks, John. I appreciate your help."

Superintendent Morrow then called his Inspectors into his office and quickly worked out an operational plan for the re-routing of traffic from Cook Island so it bypassed Brighton where the Regatta was being held and ended in a large park where Police could be waiting. He was still worried but didn't want to call his wife Kelly. He knew she would call the other mothers of the Venturers and word could easily spread to the Media about what was happening.

The lives of Scott, his Venturer Unit and the Ranger Guides could be at stake.

Chapter Twenty-Eight

The Eagles checked their panniers and took out their shotguns and rifles and loaded them. Benny led the group while Rick Lane brought up the rear. They were going Raven hunting and a new era of order on Sydney's streets was about to begin. The group rode out fast and loud with Benny's unmistakable bike with special high handles leading the pack. It was like a wolf pack on wheels about to chase down a quarry that would mean a bitter and bloody fight to the death.

Andy was still seething from what Rick and Benny had said about his two friends and the denial about the Henchmen. He weighed up in his mind what to do and decided to wait until the battle was in play before he made his move. He could take both Rick and Benny now but the resultant explosions would also kill and badly injure Eagles members who had nothing to do with Gordon and John's deaths.

The Eagles rode onto the peninsula road and started approaching two semi-trailers parked on the side of the road. Robert made a call to Ken Street as soon as the Eagles came into view. The Ravens were almost ready. The sticking point was taking the Steyer bullets from their plastic packing and passing them around. Once Rick Lane passed the trucks both heavy vehicles started up. Robert drove forward and did a

U-turn. He went back down the road and did another U-turn to head back up the peninsula road. Jim turned his vehicle side-on and jumped out. Robert drove as fast as he could and hit the second semi-trailer mid-on causing it to tip over onto its side, completely blocking the road so no traffic could come in or out. He jumped out of his rig and joined Jim as they recovered their bikes and rode along the peninsula loop road with shotguns in their hands.

Benny raised his right hand and half of the Eagles took the right fork of the road near the silent sandstone sentinel and headed towards the shops. They were going to try and trap the Ravens in a crossfire if they could. He continued down the left-hand fork. The explosion of the two trucks hitting each other could be heard resonating around the Cook Island precinct. Rick looked behind him and saw a pall of smoke rising but couldn't determine what caused it. He rode to the right and left Benny with the left flank.

Cameron was the first to surface, followed quickly by William, Scott, and Mark. Mike shepherded the rest as they made their way to the fresh air.

"Did you see Old Blue? I'm sure he recognised me," Scott yelled excitedly across the group of divers. "I thought he may have only swum near the other side of the fort's foundations. How fantastic! Eeha!" Scott said with a very noticeable change in the pitch of his voice.

The other boys started laughing and Cameron pointed to a pall of black smoke billowing from the top of the bluff.

"Looks like a problem near our cars," Cameron said as all attention was now focused on the smoke. "Everyone okay?"

All the boys and Mike signalled they were fine and Cameron returned the signal.

"Okay chaps, let's swim across this channel and back to the rocks. Our underwater ride is near an end."

The group then blew air into their buoyancy vests and started swimming across the open channel under the wooden carriageway bridge to the rocky shelf they used to dive into the water. The boys found getting into the water was easy enough, but heaving themselves onto the rocky shoreline while waves washed over them was hard. A number lost their footing as they tried to stand and fell over. Giggles and laughter punctuated the air as the boys took off their fins and stood up, helping their buddies and anyone else near them. Mike became worried as he scanned the road above the small rocky cliff line leading to the shoreline where he stood. Lined up in a row were many black-painted motorcycles and no riders to be seen. He motioned to Cameron to look skywards, and the Rover also suddenly had the wind punched out of his sails.

"Okay, guys we may have some company above. When we climb to the carriageway above, be sharp and keep a good lookout," Cameron said.

"What do you think they are doing?" Ian asked.

"Don't know. However, this is pretty unusual to have motorbikes like these parked here. The other worrying factor is the smoke Mike and I saw as we surfaced."

"Maybe the bikies are causing some hassles," William said.

"Whatever it is, the quicker we can get changed and out of here the better it will be. If we see any bikies, no comments, no looks and hopefully, no issues."

Scott's mind started racing. "Cameron, the girls are up there somewhere. Do you think they're alright?"

"Scott they should be. Everyone should be. It's just a feeling I have had come over me, that's all. Come on guys, shake a leg and let's get moving."

The boys moved with renewed vigour. They were keen to see what was happening and also to ensure the girls were safe. They clambered over the rocky shoreline and up the small hill to the carriageway in record time. If they weren't so young and fit their bodies would have had major difficulties. Mike was slightly puffing at the end as he tried to keep up with his young charges.

Rosie had heard the trucks colliding as the noise resonated around the precinct. She instinctively looked up and saw the smoke.

"Okay girls, it's time we went to Namara's. I feel a nice, iced chocolate coming on," Rosie said.

Mandy and Liane both picked up on the stress in Rosie's voice and said nothing. A look at each other was sufficient. They also had heard the collision and saw the smoke. The fact a group of bikies was in town also spelt possible trouble. Both were looking forward to meeting up with the Venturers and going home. The girls made their way up the beach and over a small bluff. To their right and up a rise along the peninsula road were their van and the boys' vehicles. To their left was a group of shops that looked deserted. Ahead of them was Namara's Café. The girls started making a bee-line towards the café when they saw several bikers with weapons in their hands lying in the grass and just below some small rock platforms that dotted a common between Namara's Café and the silent sandstone sentinel. Not a word was spoken as the girls saw the men nearby. They quickly started running towards the café.

"What the hell is that?" Tim said as he scanned the area with his binoculars.

"What do you mean? Damian asked.

"A group of girls … girl guides just ran into the café. I thought we cleared out all the civilians?"

"Oh hell. Well, they'll be safe in there for the moment. How many did you count?"

"I didn't have time to count. By the time it registered with me as to what they were, they were gone."

"No probs. We'll have to steer the Eagles away from the café."

"Okay."

Rosie and her girls made it onto the porch of the café and frantically knocked on the door. No one answered. Liane and Mandy looked to the sides of the café and saw the bikers on the common. They became quite scared. The girls decided to break all the rules if no one answered their knocks. Rosie tried knocking once more. No answer. Liane took off her pullover and put it over a pane of glass in the front door. She gave a heavy elbow push into the pullover and onto the glass, breaking the pane. Liane then reached in through the empty space until she found the front door latch and undid it. The girls poured into the café and closed and locked the door. Rosie used her mobile phone and rang the Police on the emergency 112 number. The operator put her straight through to an operations officer in the Sydney Police Centre. Rosie explained what was happening and was told to stay put. The Police would soon be there to help.

Superintendent John Giddings revelled in operational mayhem as he would try and restore order with his heavily armed and trained Police. However, the phone call about the Ranger Guides trapped in Namara's café sent shivers down his spine. He was becoming worried his worst nightmare was about to unfold. Before he could speak with his field commanders on the bus another series of calls came through on the emergency 000 landlines. Two trucks had collided at the entrance to Cook Island with one being forced on its side and on fire. His frustration grew as he saw the incidents being recorded on a large board in the Operations Room. He spoke with his tactician Inspector Barney Drover and was told the first group of Police was still a couple of minutes away from the approach to Cook Island. Drover explained the trucks were probably a ploy by one of the biker groups to stop Police and other emergency services from entering the Cook Island precinct thus allowing any skirmish to take place unchecked. It would be a while before heavy lift cranes could get to the site and move the trucks out of the way. The Police water cannon truck resembled an armoured personnel carrier but was no match for moving heavily laden trucks out of the way.

The moment the Venturers hit the carriageway they heard a metallic, throaty roar that kept getting louder and then seemed to split in origin. Mike was now very concerned about the safety of the boys and the Ranger Guides.

"What the hell is that?" Mark shouted above the roar as he looked to Mike.

"I'd say from all the bikes below and the noise above we are being visited by quite a few bikers," Mike said.

"Do you reckon they had anything to do with all that smoke we saw as we surfaced?" Scott asked.

"Why would they? It's probably just an accident somewhere. Who knows, these bikers are probably having a chapter ride out here to enjoy the sights the same as you and I."

The boys were tired. They were wearing full wetsuits with buoyancy vests, air tanks and weights. Climbing onto the rocky shoreline amid ebbing and crashing waves was one thing but almost running up a steep roadway fully kitted out was another! They made it to the top peninsula road near where their vehicles were parked. Each of them looked around to see if they could see Rosie and the girls. Cameron scanned the common, museum and café and couldn't see the girls. Their van was still parked near the Venturers' cars.

"They're probably having a hot chocolate or something in the café," Cameron said to Mike.

"I hope so. Let's get to the cars and get out of this gear, it's too restrictive," Mike said. "We also need to ring Rosie to ensure she is alright."

"No probs."

Cameron then started herding the boys like cats towards their cars. His eyes saw movement on top of the sandstone sentinel. He looked closer and saw the shape of a head moving around. Initially, no problems, except he expected the person to have been taller and more of a silhouette to be seen. While he walked to the cars he looked again and what he saw scared the hell out of him. The moving head on the sandstone sentinel had a rifle. He told the boys to run to the cars and put his hands out wide to push them along. The boys never argued with Cameron. They trusted him emphatically. They made it to the side of the cars without incident.

"What was that about?" Mike said, sidling up to Cameron.

"There's someone at the top of the tower with a rifle and I was being extremely cautious."

"Well done."

"Guys, get your gear off quickly and just put it in the rear of the cars. We'll sort it later."

Mike reached for his keys stuck by a magnet under the fender of the passenger side rear wheel. He opened his car, reached in and retrieved Cameron's keys and threw them to the Rover who quickly opened his car. The boys started stripping out of their diving gear. Before they had got too far, they heard a volley of shots being fired somewhere near the common. Instinctively Mike yelled to the boys to take cover behind the cars. The boys moved in close to each other and helped take each other's wetsuits off. A lot of shouting and more shooting could be heard from the common. Mike and Cameron reached up into their cars and retrieved their mobile phones.

"Cameron, you check with Rosie, I'll call for help," Mike said as he started punching 112 on his mobile phone. Within seconds he was taken to an emergency services operator and detailed where he was and that he was in an area where a large exchange of gunfire was taking place. The operator could hear the shots in the background as he was talking. Mike was put through straight away to the operations room of the Police Centre.

"Mike, stay calm and keep the boys out of the way," Sergeant Bud Loughry said in an even and calm voice. "We've got Police close to you and they shouldn't be too long getting to your area."

"We're okay and sort of well shielded from the firing. It's the girls we're all worried about."

"Hang on." Sergeant Loughry made some quick enquiries with other Police in the room. "Mate they're okay. They are in Namara's Café. Can you see the café from where you are?"

"Yeah, we can see the roof of it behind the museum. The ground dips down to where we are on the link road. We're almost outside the road leading down to the wooden bridge and the fort on Cook Island."

"Have you actually seen any bikers yet?"

"No, we saw more than 20 of their bikes where the road leads down from the peninsula road and joins up with the wooden bridge to the fort. It's a flat area you can't see from the top road. Also, there is an armed person in the tower. He's not standing but is keeping low. We saw him with a high-powered rifle of some sort."

"Okay, Mike. Hang up now and stay with the boys. I've got your number and will keep ringing you for updates, so the cost is mine, not yours. If something happens, ring back immediately."

"Check."

The pair rang off. The boys had not seen Mike go into his Army style of talking before as he spoke with the Police officer. They were comforted in the fact they had vehicle shields between them and the bikers as long as no one came towards them. The boys, Mike and Cameron changed into their Scout uniforms.

"This will be a dive you will never forget," Mike said to Scott as he pulled on a gym shoe.

"No. I don't think any of us ever will. It's the girls I'm worried about."

Cameron got off the phone and rejoined the group. "Rosie and the girls are okay. They had to break into Namara's Café but are all okay. They've told the Police who have ordered them to stay put."

"At least they can have a hot chocolate on the house," William said.

This sent the boys into a laugh at the thought of the girls making hot chocolates and waiting to be rescued. Cameron relaxed more as he pulled on his Rover shirt and shorts. Scott sidled up to him and put his hand on the Rover's shoulder.

"They'll be fine. I reckon this little shooting match will be finished shortly when the Police arrive."

"We'll see. Our problem is if the bikers come this way to retrieve their bikes and prefer our cars instead. We might have to move somewhere else."

The Venturers had retrieved their mobile phones. Mike instructed them not to ring their parents at this stage until it was all over, otherwise they would panic and cause massive issues trying to get their sons out. The boys agreed. Instead, they rang the Ranger Guides to ensure they were okay and offered support.

Superintendent John Giddings decided the biker situation was at an impossible stage. He had two groups of children trapped between warring bikers and wanted no more collateral damage. He ordered the Regatta to be abandoned and the crowd dispersed as fast as possible. There had been a domino effect with events so far and he didn't want it to spread to the hundreds of other children at the end of the bay. Police had arrived at the truck site but couldn't enter the peninsula road in their vehicles until heavy cranes had moved the trucks. Fire Brigade officers had reached the scene and were extinguishing the truck blaze. Ambulance crews were parked on the side roads and would not go anywhere until Police required them and had cleared the way in and out for them.

Christopher Johns received the call from the Police Operations Room to abandon the Regatta and start dispersing the crowd in an orderly fashion as soon as possible. He called his Rover organisers together and gave the instructions. His son Michael listened carefully to what was being said.

"Dad, you know that Scott Morrow is out there at Cook Island, don't you?"

"The Police will help him, don't worry about him for the moment. Our priority is to safely get these scouts and their families out of here and home."

"Scott's in trouble" the murmurs could be heard throughout the Rover crowd. "He needs help too."

Christopher Johns was taken aback. "Our priority is to get these children out of here now. Then you think about Scott Morrow. Come on, we have to get the boats in, packed and on their way in record time."

Clusters of Rovers started to climb aboard their Skidoos in a bid to herd the sailing craft to shore. Other Rovers began to get the parents organised in packing up quickly and ready to take their children home as quickly as possible when they returned to shore.

Michael Johns started to sing. He had met Scott in the morning and helped him prepare the sailboats for the Regatta. The Rovers had joined in the singing then as they competed with the leaders and parents.

Maybe it would help calm things now and get people's minds off the dangers that could be approaching, he thought. Then, as he started pulling sailboats up the shore, he sang aloud, *"One man went to mow, went to mow a meadow ..."*

One by one the Rovers looked at Michael and joined in. The singing was not joyful like the morning's rendition but kept increasing as more voices joined in. The singing was strained, deeper and more mechanical than earlier. However, it helped the Rovers as they pulled the myriad of boats to the shoreline and up onto the beach. It also kept the Scouts in the boats calm as they were stopped in their various stages of sailing.

"You know we can't leave them up there don't you," Johnathon Lalas said to a few of his other Rovers. "We have the perfect means of escape right in front of us."

"You'd have to be kidding, wouldn't you?" Dean Wicks said as he pulled a small sailing boat up the shoreline.

"No. If Scott is trapped on the peninsula road with his back to the water, then it is the water that is the perfect escape."

"Christopher said the Police would be there soon to help rescue them, why should we jump in and get ourselves possibly killed in the bargain?"

"Dean. This is Scott Morrow. He's gone out of his way to

help rescue Venturers and Rovers and now he and his Venturers need help. The National Rover Emergency Rescue Service could suddenly spring a new branch right here. We're all pretty good sailors. We grew up sailing these boats ourselves when we were Scouts, so we know the equipment and we know the bay. I say it's up to us to help out."

The other Rovers started agreeing with Johnathon. They approached Christopher and said they would look after the boats until the issue blew over. This way it would save families valuable time while they picked up their children and drove home. Christopher was not happy about what the Rovers were proposing but knew by splitting his forces he had a better chance of safely getting the Scouts and their families out of the bay area. The Rovers were adults and could choose to stay if they wished. He gave his blessing to the Rovers on the proviso they helped to clear the bay and beach line of all families. The Rovers agreed and started their work. Johnathon found Michael Johns and pulled him aside.

"Thank you, Michael," Johnathon said.

"I didn't do anything," Michael said.

"I remember being in the Blue Mountains when Scott Morrow was rescued from his canyoning trip. He said something similar. Don't worry, the Rovers are a tight band of brothers when it comes to helping each other out. Go home now and practise your singing."

The two laughed and Michael headed to his father's car and was the last Scout to leave the beach.

"Dad, will the Rovers be okay?" Michael asked as his father whisked him home.

"The Rovers will be fine. This is their turf. They know the bay better than anyone their age because of all the practice they have had sailing here too. Yes, they'll be okay."

"What about Scott and his Venturers? Do you think they'll make it?"

"It's a tough one to answer. It all depends on what is happening around Cook Island. I guess at this stage, all we can do is pray for them."

Michael closed his eyes and said a silent prayer for the Venturer he had met earlier in the day and his Unit. He was genuinely worried for them all.

Chapter Twenty-Nine

The Eagles rode either side of the peninsula road with weapons drawn. Damian fired the first shot and it went wide, taking off a mirror on Benny's bike. Benny's group pulled their bikes over and leapt to the small embankment between the road and the grassy common. A second shot rang out and grazed the side of a helmet being worn by an Eagle. A volley of shots rang out from where Benny and his team lay on the embankment. Rick Lane and his group were near the cluster of shops and quickly pulled over and ran to the embankment on their side of the road.

The Raven in the sandstone sentinel fired several shots at Benny's group. His fourth shot hit the hand of one of the bikers, smashing through the skin and bones and creating a rapid outpouring of blood. The biker rolled over in agony while his mates fired at where they thought the Ravens were firing from.

Rick Lane's group saw the Raven in the tower and aimed and shot at him. The Raven was virtually lying down with only a portion of his head visible from the lower corner of the stone cutting. He turned his attention to Rick's group and fired a small salvo. While Rick's group returned the fire on the tower a couple of new shooters were firing from near the museum. One Raven had even crept into the fenced-off grave of the French Priest who died a short time after Captain James Cook had arrived in Botany Bay. The Raven had been hiding behind the grille fence and now revealed himself by firing on the Eagles. Rick's group was almost pinned down. Rick crouched down and started moving around the embankment to get a better shot when two thuds in quick succession were heard. His screams were next as he looked at his leg and felt the searing pain where he had been shot twice in the right leg. An Eagle quickly pulled out a knife from his boot and tore Rick's jeans open. He cut a long strip of material and made a tourniquet for his club president. The tourniquet stemmed the bleeding but not the pain.

Ken Street had positioned himself near the Museum and was able to fire on both Eagles groups. The return volleys started peppering the walls of the Museum. Once the shooting had begun, Rosie had got all the girls to go to the rear of Namara's Café and lay down on the floor under tables. She cuddled the frightened Guide as shots rang out across the grassy common between the two biker groups. Rosie looked up from the floor to a painting of a beaming Namara. The owner of the café had been a Girl Guide leader and was painted telling a yarn to a group of Guides.

"Lucky you," Rosie said under her breath to Namara. "Wouldn't you like to trade places with me?" The painting never responded. The artist had painted Namara front on and her eyes seemed to follow you wherever you were in the room. Rosie would never forget Namara. The more she looked at the painting, the more she drew strength from it. Rosie's mobile phone rang amid another volley of shots.

"Rosie, don't hang up. It's Sergeant Loughry. Are you okay?"

"Yes. We're in the rear room of Namara's Café on the floor under some tables."

"Is anyone hurt?"

"No. We're okay. We're scared as all hell and frightened something is going to happen, but we're okay."

"Alright. Keep the girls calm. We're not far away now. We had a problem with a few trucks blocking our way in. We've nearly solved the issue."

"Okay. You better tell the boys that."

"We have. They're okay where they are too."

"Alright, thanks. Just remember, when you guys come in, we're the good guys in blue too!"

"No probs."

Benny's hand was strapped and he was laid down near the edge of the road. It was a dead spot where shots couldn't hit him because of the curvature of the embankment. He now had to wait this out before he could be moved. The same went for Rick.

The Ravens seemed to have the upper hand when it came to directing their fire. Their problem lay in the fact they had to unwrap the packets of bullets and then feed the magazines before loading their rifles. The Eagles mostly used shortened shotguns which had a splatter effect when fired close up, but weren't much good over distances. A couple had handguns, and these were causing the Ravens to keep their heads down.

The Raven inside the sandstone tower made a near-fatal mistake. Bullets were directed at one cutting at the top of the column forcing him to move too close to another. A single shot rang out and a yelp could be heard as the Raven was shot in the left shoulder. He laid on the ground and pulled a handkerchief from his pocket and fed it under his jacket and shirt to the wound. A few moments later he passed out from the pain.

Ken Street made one move too many as he bobbed around the entrance to the Museum. A volley of shots rang out from two separate directions with two of them nicking him on either shoulder. He ran towards Namara's Café but was turned back by two Eagles who had him in their gun sights and let loose a hail of bullets in his direction. The more he moved towards the café, the more shots were being fired at him. He decided to dash back to the Museum when another salvo rained toward him. Two bullets hit the giant gas bottle at the front of the café causing it to explode into a huge ball of flame, spewing fire all over the front of the eatery. Ken made it to the Museum and ran behind it.

Rosie and the girls screamed as they realised they were trapped in a burning building with the only exit through high windows. If they stood up, they could be gunned down. If they moved to the front of the café, they would be burned alive.

Scott and Will's mobile phones rang – it was Liane and Mandy. The boys could see fire and smoke coming from near the Museum but thought it had been hit.

"Scott, you have to get us out of here," Mandy screamed down the phone. "We can't get out of the front door because of the fire. If we climb through the windows, we'll be shot. Help us, please!" Mandy then hung up as she started to console some of the other girls.

Mike and Cameron had done their best to keep the boys near their vehicles and away from the firefight. Scott was terrified the girls would be burned alive. Will was so angry he wanted to run onto the common and try and stop the shooting. Both knew if they made a rash move they could be mincemeat with salvos of bullets hitting them.

Scott came up with an idea. He wanted to get the Australian flag out of Mike's car and use it to wave to both warring sides that he was going to save the girls. Mike and Cameron told him not to do it as it was too dangerous. Scott went quiet and looked at Will. His mate saw a way to help and pushed Scott to the rear of the Venturers. The boys closed ranks and while arguing took place between the rest of the Venturers, Mike and Cameron, Scott opened Mike's car. Brett joined him.

"Thanks for your help," Scott said.

"No probs. We have work to do."

"You realise we could get shot and killed trying to do this?"

"Yes, but if we don't make a move all those girls will surely die. I remember when a mate of mine jumped into a tree to save me. He never thought of himself or the dangers. It's my turn now to help someone else."

The boys looked at each other and smiled. Their bond of friendship was close. Being in Venturers did this to people because of the many adventures each shared with the other. Scott pulled the Australian flag from the car and started waving it high. Brett did the same with his Venturer Unit flag. Mike and the rest of the Venturers stopped yelling at each other as Scott and Brett started walking slowly forward towards the grassy common waving their flags, slowly, rhythmically. The rest of the Venturer Unit fell silent, looked at Mike and Cameron and followed the two boys. Mike and Cameron gritted their teeth but knew they couldn't stop the boys and joined the two lines of boys behind the flag bearers. The group processed slowly across the road and up the embankment onto the grassy common while several shots rang out in from of them.

Ravens and Eagles kept firing at each other sending sprays of dirt from the ground into the air or peppering the sides of buildings with their bullets. A couple of the bikers saw the boys and started yelling at them to go away with a whole host of expletives. They realised the boys were Venturers, unarmed and on a mission towards the burning Namara's Café.

"Cease fire, cease fire," a bloodied Ken Street yelled out as he saw the boys walking towards the Museum. Scott and Brett were no longer terrified or scared – they were beyond it now. They were on a mission to save the Ranger Guides and this was the only way they could do it. Gary and Andy from the Eagles yelled out to their members to stop firing, too. A lull formed on the common as the boys slowly moved past the Museum and around the blazing entrance to Namara's to the rear windows. Brett helped Scott onto his shoulders and the deft teenager used a rock to smash the window.

"Rosie, Rosie, it's alright. It's Scott. We're here to rescue you," Scott yelled.

The fire had taken a strong hold and was very noisy as it devoured the front walls and furniture of the café. Smoke had filled the café making it hard to see and breathe. Scott yelled out again and this time got a response.

"Scott is that you?" Mandy screamed.

"Yes. Quick, get the girls onto the tables and start climbing out. The bikies have a cease-fire while we get you out."

A series of screams and cheers rang out from within Namara's as the girls started to stand up. Liane and Mandy helped the young Guide out of the window first and into Scott's arms. He lowered her down to Cameron and Mike. The Venturers took it in turns to form a human pyramid and prop each other up. The same process went on getting the girls out until it was Rosie's turn.

"I can't do it Scott. I'm too big," she screamed in terror at the teenager.

"Yes you can," Scott said firmly but calmly. "We've got this far. You have to help yourself for the next part. After that, it will be plain sailing."

Rosie calmed. She looked at Namara's painting and saluted it. In a move of pure bravado for the Ranger Guide Leader, she climbed the chair and table and reached through the window to Scott. The boy was framed with the sun directly behind him. Rosie looked at Scott and never saw him. Instead, she saw an angel reaching into the window and calmly, calling her forward. It was only when she was through the wooden frame and being manhandled did she realise it was Scott. The sun had played tricks with her at this time of heightened emotion.

"Okay, I now want you all to hold each other's hands and walk slowly with us," Scott directed. "We can do it."

The Police made a breakthrough with the heavy crane

finally moving one of the semi-trailers out of the way. A fleet of Police cars was led into the area by the armoured water cannon vehicle and ringed the grassy common. Police had commandeered a fleet of small buses and these ferried in large numbers of Police. The Police stood aghast as they saw Scott and Brett waving their flags and walking slowly away from the burning café. A couple of the Police cried as they watched the innocent youths walking with the girls in what was a desperate act. The Venturers had formed a tight pack around the girls and Rosie to protect them and were walking slowly. Each of the boys walked hand in hand in a very tight ring. The Police had not been able to effect a rescue and it was left to the Venturers and lone Rover to do it.

A wind blew and the flags fluttered as the Venturers and Rangers saw the Police amid the smoke and started walking towards them. Scores of voices could be heard coming from the fort as Rovers in every sail craft they could muster from the Regatta had made their way to Cook Island. They were singing in unison as they beached their craft and started gathering on the rocky shores. They wanted to let the Venturers know their mates were on the way. The Rovers had also taken a giant leap forward in courage and rallied to help their younger friends in the Venturers. It was a very moving sight. A dozen well-armed Police met the Rovers as they made their way up the winding road from the fort's carriageway and past the long row of motorcycles.

"One man went to mow, went to mow a meadow ..." rang out as the Rovers sang in unison.

The Rangers and Venturers were emotional. They

automatically responded to the Rovers and joined in the singing, at first weakly and then strongly as they came nearer to the Police.

"*... one man and his dog, Spot, went to mow a meadow ...*"

Several heads started appearing on the road leading from the fort as the singing became intense. Police Officers corralled the Rovers as they went to join Scott and the Ranger Guides. The Rovers had arrived in time to see Scott and Brett walking into the arms of the Police as they waved their flags high and sang. Huge palls of smoke billowed from behind as Namara's Café was fully incinerated. It was the scene of a war movie – only it was real and involved teenagers whose courage had been tested under immense adverse conditions where their lives could have been snuffed out so quickly with a wayward shot from a shortened shotgun or a semi-automatic rifle.

Mandy quickly wrapped her arms around Scott and held him tight. Liane did the same with Will. Rosie went into a tirade of expletives as she was still shocked by the fire at Namara's Café. Several Ravens tried to make a run for it towards their bikes and out to the fort, boat and freedom only to be met by a solid wall of black-clad heavily armed police in flak jackets with automatic weapons trained on them. Eagles members had tried to make a run for it to their bikes or the shops only to be met by a cordon of heavily armed Police. Suddenly two large explosions, one on either side of the common, shattered the silence as two motorcycles blew apart, sending shrapnel for many metres. Balls of flame engulfed the remains of the vehicles. Ken and Rick turned their heads in the direction of the explosions and saw their own bikes being blown apart in balls of fire and smoke. Andy took his gloved fingers off the remote controls in his hand and quietly dropped them on the ground, kicking them away from himself. The moment the explosions ripped apart the motorcycles the Police went to the ground and their weapons waved from side to side as the officers tried to find a target that was attacking them. None were found. Cautiously they stood up. The Venturers and Ranger Guides had ducked down when they heard the explosions and also gingerly stood up. Police quickly ushered the girls into waiting cars and drove them to ambulances outside the entrance to Cook Island's ring road where the semi-trailers had now been fully pushed out of the way.

The game was now up. The bikers threw down their weapons and raised their hands. Police were quick to order the bikers to lie on the ground with their hands behind their heads and started attaching plastic cable ties to the biker's hands like handcuffs. The round-up of bikers continued along with the Raven in the tower and wounded bikers Ken Street, Rick Lane and Benny. Once the area was secure, ambulances and fire brigade units were called in to assist.

The Rovers weren't finished yet. One of them sidled up to a Police Commander and gave him a gift.

"I hope you don't mind, but we sort of found these spark plug leads from the boat moored at the wharf near the fort," he said as he handed over the leads.

"Well, that would have stopped a major problem. Well done," the Commander said as he took possession of the leads.

The Rovers weren't finished yet. They hoisted each of the Venturers, Mike and Cameron onto their shoulders and walked out to the Police communications bus. The Rovers formed a ring around the Venturers and gave them a very large B-R-A-V-O-O-O. Police and Ambulance officers stopped what they were doing as they watched the Rovers salute the Venturers for their courage under fire.

The Ranger Guides were deemed okay by Ambulance Officers and pushed their way through the Rover ring. They formed their own circle around the Venturers and gave them a B-R-A-V-O-O. They then rushed up to the boys and gave them hugs and kisses. The Rovers and rescue workers broke out into applause and cheers and the smiles on the boys said it all. They had worked as a team, not wilted under pressure and as one, became a rescue unit under extreme life-threatening conditions. The ALMs detectives arrived in time to watch the Rovers and Rangers give the Venturers their special thanks.

"Allan and Kelly will be very proud of young Scott," Detective Adams said as the three officers got out of their car.

"Yeah. He'd make a good fireman," Detective Lee responded. "Our intelligence officers on the hill overlooking this place said they watched closely with binoculars as Scott and his mate carried their flags to the burning café. He didn't even seem to flinch climbing up along his mate to get the other kids out of that inferno."

"I think any service that young man enters will be very thankful indeed," Detective Michaels said. "Luke, you better let Scott's dad know he is okay. He's been trying to get here for the last hour but was ordered to stay away by the Deputy Commissioner, on pain of death."

Detective Adams saw the humour in what his compatriot

had just said. "Methinks, I should make the call now and then we can start tidying up our little ring of bikers."

Police vans were called forward to take the various bikers to the Sydney Police Centre. They were escorted by heavily armed Police in front and at the rear. The Police Centre was the only place big enough to accommodate the two warring biker groups during interviews. Teams of forensic Police and new recruits were called to the peninsula link road. They slowly walked, and in parts crawled, through the grassy common looking for evidence of the firefight and taking dozens of photographs of the scene. A large haul of weapons was found including the Steyer rifles; unused ammunition, shortened shotguns, handguns and knives. Two electronic remote keys, similar to those used for electric garage doors were among the pile of evidence.

Ambulance crews worked on four bikers for gunshot wounds and took them to the hospital under a heavy Police guard. Three fire brigade crews worked on extinguishing the blaze at Namara's Café but were unsuccessful in saving the old wooden building. They did save the nearby Museum and prevented the fire from spreading.

Within an hour of the biker arrest wrap-up, Premier Barry Harris and Police Commissioner Rex Small called a news conference at Police Headquarters. The Police Media team had been working overtime to generate information about the biker war and the turnout of Reporters, photographers and videographers were unprecedented.

Premier Harris started the conference by praising the efforts of the Police for their work in preventing a major biker gang war from spreading into the wider community where innocent people could have been killed and maimed. He then went on to praise Scott Morrow.

"I want to pay particular attention to the efforts of a group of Venturer Scouts led by the Australian Youth of the Year, Scott Morrow, who rescued a group of Ranger Guides from a burning building while Police were trapped outside the area by overturned semi-trailers.

"These brave teenagers used our national flag and the flag of their Venturer Unit to force the bikers to cease fire while the boys went to Namara's Café, which was well alight, and rescued the Ranger Guides and their leader.

"Scott is well known to Australia for his work in rescuing his Venturers last Christmas from a group of Russian Mafia who took the boys and their leader prisoner in an old convict jail. In a move that can best be described as something only the brave dare, Scott escaped and turned the lighthouse into a weapon against the Russians.

"Earlier this year, Scott was instrumental in assisting our emergency services through the establishment of the National Rover Emergency Rescue Service to help people like Scouts who undertake adventurous activities in the wild if misadventure befalls them.

"While canyoning in the Blue Mountains, Scott saved two people in very unfortunate circumstances. One of those people, Brett, carried his Unit flag today to help bring about the biker ceasefire and rescue of the Ranger Guides.

"This whole affair today has been a rite of passage for a young man who deserves his community's thanks once again."

Commissioner Small backed Premier Harris with his praise of Scott, Brett and the rest of the Venturers, the Rover and their leader. He detailed how the boys had made a major decision to put their own lives on the line to save the Ranger Guides and their leader who were trapped in a burning building with no way out because of the shooting match between the opposing biker gangs. He also cautioned anyone ever trying something similar as it was so dangerous.

The Media asked a lot of questions about the lack of early Police response; whether the shootout was connected to the earlier car bombing. Also, whether the two bikes that exploded at Cook Island, were somehow connected to the car bombing. Commissioner Small went into detail about the car bombing now that the biker war had taken place. He emphasised no real connection had been made between the car bombing and the bike bombings, yet. The Media conference went on for around twenty minutes before Premier Harris called a halt to allow him and the Commissioner to continue with their work. He asked the Media to allow the Rangers and Venturers their privacy for a while so they could be consoled by their families after the momentous events of the day.

Premier Harris had asked Commissioner Small to gather the Venturers, Ranger Guides and their parents in his office before they went home. Police asked Mike, Cameron, Rosie and both the boys and girls to follow them to the city under escort. Each Venturer and Ranger Guide was asked to ring their parents and Police cars from all the various areas where the Venturers lived, and escorted parents to the city too, for a tearful reunion. Counsellors were called in by the Premier's office and asked to be on hand for the teenagers and their parents. Rosie called Chegs and asked her to join her and the girls at the Police Centre meeting.

All the teenagers needed to have counsellors available to talk through their visit to Cook Island and the sudden eruption of violence that overtook the joy of their respective outings. The scores of Rovers who ran the sailing Regatta and sailed their small armada to Cook Island to support Scott and his Venturers held their own parade. They sailed their craft back through Botany Bay in two lines with a single craft out front. A bright red Rover flag was flying atop the lead craft's main sail. Within two hours of the news flashes about the biker war and the arrests, Scout parents returned to the foreshore to help the Rovers. They lined the foreshore and burst into spontaneous applause as the flotilla came within earshot of the Rovers.

A lone Scout in full uniform and carrying a green Scout flag went in front of the applauding crowd, stood to attention and saluted the Rovers. Parents came forward and helped pull the boats ashore. The Rovers were all smiles and formed a circle around the Scout. They took their lead from Daniel, the Regatta organiser.

"Crews, alert," he yelled out. "We have someone special to greet us."

The Rovers came to attention.

"Crews salute."

Each of the Rovers formed the three-finger Scout salute and returned the salute of Michael Johns – the lone Scout. The Rovers broke off, closed in around Michael and picked him up and placed him on Daniel's shoulders.

"Michael, thank you for reminding us today of the value of singing while we worked," Daniel said out loud so all could hear.

"It was your prompting about Scott Morrow that also brought us together in an armada this bay hasn't seen in a long time. I can tell you, we were all there after Scott and his Venturers saved the Ranger Guides.

"We saw bravery today that will live on long in our minds well after we leave Rovers.

"If we can take a leaf out of anyone's book today it is from Scott's for his courage under extreme circumstances. Also, to you Michael Johns for helping to organise a secondary rescue party for our Venturers and Ranger Guides. Well done Michael! You became a beacon for us today in a sea of despair as you spurned us all on. Thank you."

Michael felt a familiar hand gently rub his leg and then saw his father Christopher standing beside him giving him silent support. The youth was touched by the outpourings of the Rovers and pushed back an emotional surge running through his body like an electric charge.

"Daniel, I had a good teacher – Scott Morrow. I had a good talk with him today as we helped set up the sailboats and he inspired me quite a lot," Michael said.

"I wanted to be here when you returned from helping Scott and the Venturers to let you know Scouts are also very appreciative of your help. We need our Rovers!"

Daniel started it and the rest of the Rovers joined in singing: "WELL DONE, MICHAEL. WELL DONE, MICHAEL. WELL DONE, MICHAEL."

Two of the Rovers then took Michael off Daniel's shoulders and held his feet and arms. They threw him up into the air and caught him on the way down and stood him upright. Several Rovers ruffled Michael's hair and started laughing as they told him 'job well done.'

Daniel walked back to the shoreline to his sailboat. He turned to his offsider, Steve, another Rover and nodded towards Michael.

"We'll have to watch Michael. He's another Scott Morrow in the making."

"Yes. It's refreshing to know there is a change in the style of Venturers we are getting these days."

"Ahh, but one Scott Morrow is enough."

"No Daniel. I think the world needs more Scott Morrows – someone who thinks of others and is not afraid to stand up and be counted."

"You're right. We'll have to include Michael's Troop in our visit plan."

"Now, that will be real easy."

"What do you mean?"

"Michael is about to go up to Venturers and he told me today he's decided to join Scott's Unit. We already have pretty close ties with that Unit through Cameron!"

Both Rovers nodded and laughed as they started stripping their craft in preparation for transport back to the scout hall.

Chapter Thirty

Superintendent Allan Morrow was relieved to receive a call from Detective Luke Adams. He had just been permitted to stand down by the Deputy Commissioner and to hand over the Highway Patrol part of Operation Marla to his own second in command so he could be with Scott. His son would need some support now the latest nightmare was over. Allan knew what to expect from the Media and dreaded the next few days. On another note, he was quite excited with the news Detective Adams gave him of what Scott had done. Inspector Morrow had fought back tears as the Detective neighbour described the scene that greeted the ALMs detectives.

"Allan it was truly a sight to see," Detective Adams said.

"The café was fully alight and huge flames could be seen all around the front of it. Walking towards the line of Tactical Response Group Police across the common was a tight ring of Venturers with the Ranger Guides and their leader in between them.

"Two boys were holding and waving flags out the front. Scott was one of them and Brett, the kid he saved in that canyon disaster, was the other. No one else moved. The bikies were taken back by the actions of the kids and stopped firing at each other. They obviously didn't want the blood of the kids on their hands and were probably as taken aback as we were.

"Allan, it was spellbinding as the only sounds that could be heard all came from the burning café and those two flags held by Scott and Brett, fluttering in the breeze. Once the boys reached us the bikers tried to make a run for it, but we had their escape routes covered off and outnumbered them quite considerably.

"It was almost pathetic how quick they gave themselves up. The scariest thing was the explosions of two bikes as the bikers were being arrested."

Allan had listened to all Detective Adams said and soaked up the verbal description of Scott's actions. He was so proud of Scott. However, he also knew he almost lost him today. If fate didn't favour the brave, Scott could have died in a hail of bullets because of some biker turf war.

"Luke, thanks for the update. He must take after his mother. You wouldn't find me doing that sort of thing," Superintendent Morrow said.

"Well, now here's the rub. We all reckon the same."

The two men laughed and rang off. Allan had to go to the city and link up with his wife Kelly who he knew from the police radio, was being taken to the Premier's office. The journey through the outer suburbs took an eternity. Allan wanted to put his siren on and drive at breakneck speed through the traffic. However, he knew this feeling was only an adrenalin rush and would soon subside. He was around twenty minutes behind the Venturers reaching the tall building overlooking Sydney Harbour the Premier called his office. Allan found parking easy in his Police car and made his way into the lift and up to the top floor. The scene was electric. Mike and the Venturers, Rosie and her Ranger Guides were being hugged and spoken to by the parents. Civilians Allan knew to be Counsellors, were mingling with the teenagers and parents to see if they wanted any assistance. Across the room he found his blonde-haired son Scott staring at him. The two met with their eyes before the youth waved and started walking towards him. Scott put his arms out and the pair embraced as Kelly made her way to join her men. She hugged them both.

Scott was relatively fine up to now. Once he saw his father, he knew he could release the pent-up emotions inside him and started crying. Allan hugged him tightly and felt his son's tears fall on his neck.

"Sorry dad," Scott said. "I had to do it. They were going to die and there was no one to help."

"Mate, it's okay. You did what you had to do. I'm so proud of you. Are you okay?"

"Yeah. This was worse than fighting with the Russians and trying to get out of that silly canyon with a busted leg."

"Why?"

"Because those men had no regard for anyone. They just kept shooting and shooting. I knew if I didn't do something Mandy, Rosie and the others would die. It wasn't fair. It just wasn't fair."

Scott released his father and stepped back to wipe his eyes, saw the tear splash marks on his father's uniform and tried to wipe them away. His father stopped him gently.

"What wasn't fair?"

"This was going to be our first outdoors picnic with the Ranger Guides and Rosie. The Venturers were really keen to have a lot of fun. Instead, we came out of the water into the middle of a shooting match. The girls had retreated into the café and then became trapped inside. Someone shot the huge gas bottle out the front and the whole place exploded.

"Dad it was terrible. We all thought the girls had died. The shooting just continued. Those bikers didn't care the girls were inside a burning building. I asked Mike to help but he said no – it was too dangerous.

"Brett and I decided to go anyway and do our best to rescue them."

"Whose idea was it for the flags?"

"Mine. I figured I needed something large for the bikers to see that would grab their attention. It worked."

"It must have been scary for you."

"I started walking up the road by myself and then Brett joined me. I felt pretty good then. Within a few moments, the whole Unit joined us including Mike and Cameron. They were so brave."

"Scott you were all so brave. Your mother and I nearly lost you today. Don't forget that. You could have been taken away from us."

Scott bowed his head and started crying again.

"I'm sorry. I had to do it. The girls would have died."

Allan and Kelly put their arms around Scott again and hugged him. The trio was all crying as they came to grips with Scott's emotional release. Mike and Cameron had watched the Morrows from a few metres away. Both independently wiped their eyes as they welled up with tears. They too had had a scary day. The hardest part was not physically stopping Scott and Brett as they started their march to Namara's Café. Instead, they joined the Venturers in full support come hell or high water.

Rosie was being comforted by Chegs as parents hugged and kissed their daughters. This adventure was way off the Guiding scale for fun.

"You did well to keep the girls together and keep them calm," Chegs told Rosie. "Well done. As we say in Guiding, *Bravissimo.*"

Refreshments were brought into the room and a small lectern was placed in the corner. The teenagers and their parents started eating the beautifully made sandwiches and cakes. Tea, coffee and soft drinks were also brought out by staffers.

Premier Harris and Commissioner Small came into the room flanked by a man in scout uniform and a woman in Girl Guide uniform. Allan recognised the man as the State's top Commissioner for Venturers. He had been at both Government Houses when Scott received his bravery award and Australian Youth of the Year. He didn't recognise the Guide Leader.

"Ladies and gentlemen, Venturers and Ranger Guides, welcome," the Premier said.

"I know it has been a very trying day and I appreciate you want to go home and be with your families. Shortly. I wanted to ensure you had complete privacy away from the Media for this very special family get-together and have Counsellors available for you."

A round of applause broke out as groups of parents said "hear, hear," in support.

"I also want to say thank you to each of the Venturers and their leaders on behalf of the New South Wales Government for the wonderful display of bravery and courage under fire you all showed in rescuing the Ranger Guides and their leader.

"Each one of you could have been killed today through your actions. Instead, by a special act of bravado and daring do, you stopped one of Sydney's worst turf wars. In doing so, you brought yourselves and your organisations into strong focus nationally.

"On my way here tonight I had a telephone call from Prime Minister Robert Anthony. He wanted me to pass on his personal congratulations and that of the national government to the boys for saving the lives of the Ranger Guides and their leader. Well done.

"He was particularly pleased Scott hadn't placed him in a position to call out the Commandos and their Blackhawk helicopter again."

Scott and the rest of the audience laughed and clapped. The Premier was referring to when Brett was badly injured in an abseiling accident during the Unit's canyoning trip earlier in the year, the Prime Minister authorised Commandos in a Blackhawk helicopter to assist with the rescue.

Cameron couldn't hold back any longer. "Mr Premier, don't forget it was the Rovers who stopped any potential getaway by the bikers with their boat. They also took a flotilla through Botany Bay to assist the Venturers and Ranger Guides."

The Premier smiled as a minder leant forward and spoke quietly to him.

"Cameron, the Rovers also need our vote of thanks today for what they did. Not only did they clear Botany Bay of any potential threat to hundreds of people including many children, but they also set out on a special voyage to save their compatriots in Venturing and Guiding. A fantastic effort and one that needs applauding."

The room erupted into applause and a series of catcalls saying "Well done Rovers, well done."

Mike put his arm on Cameron's shoulder and patted him as he thanked him for speaking up.

The Premier resumed his speech. "With me tonight are some people you may or not know from Scouting and Guiding who want to say some words to you privately."

The Premier introduced the State Commissioner for Guides, Mrs Faith Ledgard. The lady was dressed immaculately in a blue Guide hat, a blouse with little figures of Girl Guides all over it, a blue blazer, blue skirt, stockings and blue shoes.

"Good evening all. I wanted to make a special trip in to see you away from the glare of publicity to let you know how grateful the Guiding movement is to Mike, Cameron and the Venturers today. You showed the world what fine young men Scouting can produce in its purest sense by your deeds today.

"I firmly believe if Lord Baden-Powell was alive today, he would be so proud of you. The same would also apply to our founder, Lady Olave Baden-Powell. Words cannot accurately express the gratitude Guiding has for each of her new knights in blue and maroon uniforms."

Brett looked at Cameron and yelled out: "Don't forget the Rovers."

"Thank you, Brett. I was coming to them to also thank Cameron and Mike Hunter for the parts they played in supporting you through what can only be described as one of the most dangerous acts of bravery we have seen in this country in a long time. The phones at Guide headquarters and the senior leadership group went into virtual meltdown this afternoon with hundreds of calls from Ranger Guides, leaders, parents and community leaders trying to find out about the girls and offering support.

"Thank you from all the Girl Guides and their leaders. Keep up your good work in Scouting. God bless."

The room erupted into very strong applause and cat calling of 'thank you.'

The top Commissioner for Venturers in the State Anthony Soames was next at the lectern. "Faith, on behalf of the Venturers and their families, Mike and Cameron, thank you.

"We don't praise our teenage boys enough in this country for the wonderful things they can do when circumstances dictate. Today is one of those days when we heap praise on our youth for a fantastic job. Well done. You had the picture painted from Faith of both our organisation's founders giving their blessing for your actions today. Please know that Guide headquarters was not alone in a phone meltdown. Not only did we have to call in extra operators to field calls about your deeds today but also bring in a couple of webmasters to handle the near-complete shutdown of our State and national websites due to unprecedented e-mail traffic.

"We had an avalanche of hits from around the world wanting to know whether you survived today and what you will do next. Also, what happened to the Ranger Guides and their leader. I also have messages from the National and State Commissioners for Scouting congratulating you on a job well done. They also emphasised for me to tell you: please don't do it again. We love you as young fun people seeking adventure, not what could have become of you had any stray or direct bullets found their marks with you!"

The room applauded again in support of the Commissioner.

Premier Harris then said he would talk to each of the teenagers before offering everyone a ride home in a Police car if they needed one. The Premier, Police Commissioner, and Guiding and Venturer Commissioners worked the room talking to each of the boys and girls, their parents, Mike, Cameron, and Rosie.

When it came Scott's turn to talk with the Premier, Kelly put her arm around her son's waist and stood close.

"You know Scott, I truly meant it today when I said you had undergone a rite of passage with your actions."

"I'm not quite with you. What do you mean?"

"Scott, this State and country have watched you grow into a young man. Today you went past being the youth who saved his mates and leader from the drug-running Russian Mafia in a lighthouse. You went further than the young man who saved his best mate in a dangerous abseiling accident while canyoning. Today, a man stood up to be counted when he realised there was no one else who could help. You also inspired the rest of your Unit, Mike and Cameron to join you in a desperate act to save the Ranger Guides and their leader. Those of us that have been watching you saw you transition into a man today in a special rite of passage."

"Thank you, Mr Premier. My parents and Mike Hunter always taught me to do my best and to try hard no matter how hard things got. When I realised the girls had no way of escape and the bikers either didn't know the girls were trapped or didn't care, I had to act. I was lucky the rest of the Unit, Mike and Cameron backed me. I was pretty scared, I can tell you."

The Premier smiled broadly and shook Scott's hand and those of his parents before moving on to speak with Brett and his parents. Scott was hugged by both Kelly and Allan.

A lot of tears flowed from all those in the Premier's office before they left to resume their lives. It was a day and a night all would remember for the rest of their lives.

The subsequent investigation by the ALMs detectives into the Eagles' murders cleared Eagles members Jim Harris and Freddy O'Mara of the murders of Gordon Bennett and John Roberts. Rick Lane and Benny were charged with a string of offences including procuring agents to murder Gordon Bennett and John Roberts. More than forty bikers from the Ravens and Eagles Motorcycle Clubs were charged with affray; attempted murder and various firearm offences.

No one was found guilty of the firebombing murders of the Henchman and their vehicle or the bombing of Rick Lane's and Benny's motorcycles. The State Government cleared a small prison and put all the convicted bikers together to serve their sentences which ranged from two years to life imprisonment.

Calm was restored around Kings Cross with the demise of

the Ravens and Eagles Motorcycle Clubs. Shopkeepers could once again go about their business with the confidence they could prosper.

The ALMs detectives were deemed so successful as a team they were assigned together with Luke Adams reaching the rank of Inspector within a year. Superintendent McPherson retired but acted as a consultant to the Commissioner.

Epilogue

The day after Rosie and her girls were rescued from the fire at Namara's Café, they held a meeting in their guide hall with Chegs. The Region Leader introduced State Commissioner Faith Ledgard to the girls and their parents.

"Ladies and families. You have been through hell and back. I want you to know the National Guide Commissioner and I have both prayed to God thanking him for your safe return.

"You were lucky you had teamed up with some truly remarkable young men in the form of Venturers. They put their lives on the line to save you from a fiery inferno that was ready to engulf you. They helped stop a major shooting war between two biker groups that could have claimed all your lives. I am a true believer in God and I firmly believe you were protected by your guardian angels and the boys to have come through unscathed. We have some work to do together as we look at ways to improve our training and programs for Guides and Ranger Guides to update them and so encourage more wonderful people like you into our organisation."

Mrs Ledgard spoke to Rosie and each of the girls privately to see if they needed anything and then left. After the meeting when everyone had gone home, Rosie and the Ranger Guides were asked for interviews by the Media. Rosie called on Mike Hunter to act as their Media go-between.

Scott featured prominently in the Media again as a national hero. However, he and Mike pushed hard for recognition of the rest of the Unit and the Rovers for standing up to be counted when the time called for it. This helped deflect some of the attention away from Scott.

Within a few days, Rosie and Scott received some odd mail. Rosie received a note from the Post Office that a parcel was waiting for pick up. She had not ordered anything but went to satisfy her curiosity. The postmaster went into a back room and returned with a large rectangular parcel that had a letter attached to the front. Rosie read the letter and broke into tears.

"Dear Anne or "Rosie" as I know your girls call you.

I received a call from Faith Ledgard after your heroic time in my café. I understand from Faith you gained an inner strength to keep your sanity and that of the girls under the most distressing of pressure from my special painting as my café was burning and the bikers were conducting a turf war outside on the common.

Artist Phillip Jamieson had a daughter in my Guide Unit and was so thankful for the wonderful stories she shared with him about her adventures with the Guides and me that he painted the beautiful work you now know so well.

I had the painting framed and hung in my Guide Hall until I retired and then moved it to my home. I loved the work so much that I had a print made of it and had it hung in Namara's Café. So many people enjoyed the print I had to leave it there. It's now time to give joy and hope to a new generation of Guides.

I have sent you the original painting in the hope you and other leaders like you, and the next generation of Guides may also draw strength from it."

Yours in Guiding,

'Namara'

May Sullivan

Rosie peeked inside the wrapper and saw the haunting eyes of Namara looking out as she was happily talking to a group of Guides. She put the painting down and started crying again. The postmaster came out from behind his counter, put his hand gently on her shoulder and she held it until she calmed. Rosie thanked the man and went home and rang Mike Hunter. Within the hour the pair was in her Guide hall where Mike hung the painting. The couple stood back to admire it and Rosie instinctively placed her hand around Mike's waist. He automatically did the same and the couple leant their heads towards each other until they gently touched while they viewed the painting. It was an emotional moment and Mike was glad he was invited to share it with a woman he really admired.

Scott received a large letter in the post. Inside the plain envelope was a second envelope. This one had a special cypher in the top left-hand corner he had seen before. It was a sprig of wattle with a crown on top and the words "Office of the Governor General of Australia" written on it. Scott was amused His Excellency had used subterfuge to send a private letter to him. He was also hoping this was not another invitation to an awards ceremony.

> *Private and Confidential*
> *"Dear Scott,*
>
> *I was personally moved by your heroic actions on the weekend in the rescue of the Ranger Guides and their leader from a burning building amid a major shootout by biker gangs.*
>
> *Congratulations on another job well done. I know you did it without thinking of yourself and without worrying about the consequences. I also know your goal was to save the girls and not seek glory for yourself or others. Well done on carrying out such a selfless act.*
>
> *Prime Minister Robert Anthony also sends his congratulations on your heroic actions. He wants you to know he will soon be inviting you and your family to a private dinner at The Lodge to talk with you in person.*
>
> *Your actions tell me you have kept the promise you made me at Yarralumla. Well done!*
>
> *Keep up the good work. You are a credit to Australian youth everywhere."*
>
> *Your friend,*
> *Monte Brereton*
> *Governor General of Australia*

Scott was blown away. The Governor General, the man who holds the top post in the country writes to him personally and signs off as 'your friend'. How fantastic the Governor-General remembered the last time the pair had met at Government House. Scott was on crutches after rescuing Brett during the canyoning trip and went to Yarralumla, the Governor–General's official residence in the country's capital, to receive the award of Australian Youth of the Year from him. After the ceremony, the Governor-General had a private talk with Scott in his gardens. He asked Scott to continue to do his best, no matter how hard things got for him in life. Scott said he would, and he would also place his scouting skills at the disposal of the community as he promised when he received his Queens Scout Award.

Allan and Kelly Morrow shook their heads in disbelief when Scott told them of the letter. They read it and then each gave him a big hug and congratulated him.

Glossary of Terms & Characters

A Rite Of Passage   A series of events that mark a change to the status of a person, like puberty, maturing, and marriage. A time when someone stands up to be counted in an act of selfless bravery.

Allan Morrow   Scott's father.

ALMs team   NSW Police team comprising Detectives Luke Adams, Jason Lee and Simon Michaels.

Anne Hinchley   Ranger Guide Leader. Guiding name of Rosie.

Andy Hill   Member of Eagles Motorcycle Club.

Anthony Soames   NSW Commissioner for Venturers.

ANZAC Day   Special day celebrated throughout Australia on 25 th of April to commemorate wars Australians have served and died in.

Barry Harris   NSW Premier.

Barney Drover   NSW Police tactician.

Benny James   Sergeant at Arms with Eagles Motorcycle Club.

Brett   Venturer with 1ˢᵗ Hurstville Venturer Unit.

Bud Loughry   NSW Police Operations Room Sergeant.

Cameron Wagstaff   Rover with St George Rover Crew.

Centenary Sailing

Regatta   Annual Scout sailing event in Botany Bay.

Chantelle   Girl Guide.

Chapter   Branch of a motorcycle club.

Christopher Johns   Scout Michael John's father.

Chegs   District Guide Leader.

Cook Island   Former military fort in Botany Bay.

Cosh   Flexible instrument used as a bludgeon.

Damian   Member of Ravens Motorcycle Club.

Dean Wicks   Rover with St George Rover Crew.

Emergency cell phone

Number 112   In Australia the emergency number for help on a cell phone is 112.

Faith Ledgard   State Commissioner for Guides.

Freddy O'Mara   Member of Eagles Motorcycle Club.

Gary Herdman   Member of Eagles Motorcycle Club.

Geoff	Member of Ravens Motorcycle Club.
Gordon Bennett	Member of Eagles Motorcycle Club.
Henchmen	Henchmen Motorcycle Club based in Adelaide.
Hugh	Member of Henchmen Motorcycle Club.
Ian	Venturer with 1st Hurstville Venturer Unit.
Jason Lee	NSW Police Detective.
John Giddings	NSW Police Tactical Response Commander.
John Roberts	Member of Eagles Motorcycle Club.
Johnathon Lalas	Rover with St George Rover Crew.
Jim Harris.	Member of Ravens Motorcycle Club.
Keith	Member of Henchmen Motorcycle Club.
Ken Street	President of Ravens Motorcycle Club.
Kelly Morrow	Scott's mother.
Liane	Ranger Guide.
Luke Adams	Police Detective.
Mandy	Ranger Guide.
Mark	Venturer with 1st Hurstville Venturer Unit.
Melissa	Wife of murdered Eagles Motorcycle Club member John.

Michael Johns	Scout.
Michelle	Wife of murdered Eagles Motorcycle Club member Gordon.
Mike Hunter	Venturer Leader of 1st Hurstville Venturers.
Monte Brereton	Governor General of Australia.
Mitchell Gallard	Head of Henchmen Motorcycle Club members in Sydney.
Namara	Former Girl Guide Leader. Owner of Namara's Café.
National Rover Emergency Rescue Service	A national emergency rescue service run by Rovers.
NSW	New South Wales, a State within Australia
Old Blue	Giant groper found around Cook Island.
Operation Marla	NSW Police operation involved a shootout between Ravens and Eagles Motorcycle Club members.
PADI	Professional Association of Diving Instructors
Paul Hanlon	Rover with St George Rover Crew.
Paul McPherson	NSW Police Detective Superintendent in charge of the Motorcycle Gang Squad.

Peter	Venturer Unit Chairman.
Peter Sullivan	NSW Police helicopter co-pilot.
Rachel	Works in the dive shop.
Rebecca	Ranger Guide.
Rex Small	NSW Police Commissioner.
Rick Lane	President of Eagles Motorcycle Club.
Robert	Member of Ravens Motorcycle Club.
Robert Anthony	Australian Prime Minister.
Rod	Ravens Motorcycle Club member.
Roger	Ravens Lieutenant to Ken Street.
Rosie	Miss Anne Hinchley. Ranger Guide Leader.
Rovers	Scouts aged 17 to 26.
Russian Mafia	Russian gangsters tried to smuggle a large haul of drugs into Australia.
Scott Morrow	Venturer with 1st Hurstville Venturer.
Simon Michaels	NSW Police Detective.
Skip	Owner of the dive shop.
Sitrep	Situation report.
Stuart Somers	NSW Police helicopter pilot.
Ted	Member of Ravens Motorcycle Club.
The Lodge	Australian Prime Minister's official residence in Canberra.
Theo	Greek nightclub owner in Kings Cross.

Tim	Member of Ravens Motorcycle Club.
Trevor	Member of Ravens Motorcycle Club.
Venturers	Scouts aged 14 to 18.
Wobbegongs	Small sharks.

About the Author

 Christopher J. Holcroft is the author of six books. His background is in communications, media training, complex public information planning and implementation, and journalism.

He was a member of the Australian Army Reserve for more than 43 years. His overseas deployments have included Bougainville (1999), East Timor (2001), and Iraq (2006).

For more than 36 years, Christopher has been involved in scouting, including Venturer Scout Units in both Victoria and NSW. Christopher was presented the Silver Wattle Award by Scouts Australia in August 2008 for his outstanding service to Scouting. He was later awarded the Silver Koala in 2016 for his distinguished service.

Christopher holds a Masters degree in Organisational Communication from Charles Sturt University and a Bachelor of Arts degree from the University of Technology, Sydney, where he majored in Journalism and Communications Technology. He is also a Justice of the Peace.

He is married to Yvonne and the couple has three sons. They live in NSW and enjoy outdoor recreational activities including camping, abseiling and scuba diving.

www.ingramcontent.com/pod-product-compliance
Lightning Source LLC
Chambersburg PA
CBHW031941240626
47153CB00003B/813